INSPECTOR STERLING
CASE OF THE EMERALD DAGGER

PALMETTO
PUBLISHING
Charleston, SC
www.PalmettoPublishing.com

Copyright © 2024 by Reverend Dave Clements

All rights reserved

No portion of this book may be reproduced, stored in a retrieval system, or transmitted in any form by any means–electronic, mechanical, photocopy, recording, or other–except for brief quotations in printed reviews, without prior permission of the author.

Paperback ISBN: 9798822967939

INSPECTOR STERLING
CASE OF THE EMERALD DAGGER

**REVEREND
DAVE CLEMENTS**

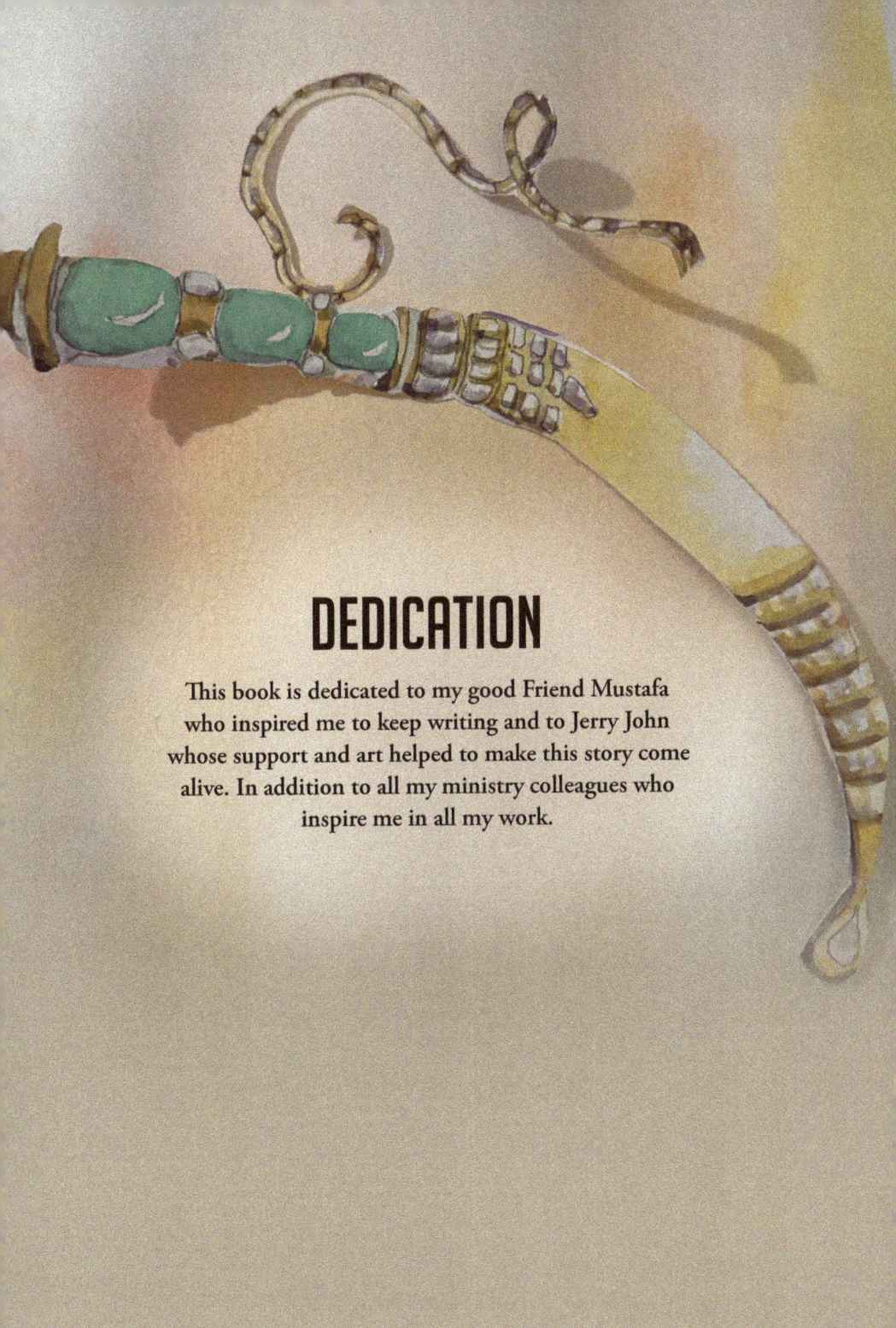

DEDICATION

This book is dedicated to my good Friend Mustafa who inspired me to keep writing and to Jerry John whose support and art helped to make this story come alive. In addition to all my ministry colleagues who inspire me in all my work.

PROLOGUE

WHO IS INSPECTOR STERLING, AND WHAT HAS HE BEEN UP TO RECENTLY?

The inspector, Charles Anthony Sterling, was born on May 20, 1963, in Glen Ellen, Illinois. When he was five, his parents moved to Peoria, Illinois. The inspector attended and graduated from St. Vincent de Paul Catholic High School in 1981. Inspector Sterling obtained a BA in political science from Ohio State in 1985 and went on and earned a master's degree in international relations from Ohio State University in 1990.

Inspector Sterling, upon graduation, started a career with the Foreign Service, and after three years of living and working in South Africa, he returned to the States and took a job with the Central Intelligence Agency. He left the CIA in April of 1996 to join the Chicago Police Department. In 1998, he was promoted to the rank of detective and assigned a role in the burglary division of the department. In 1999, Sterling volunteered to take over a murder case deemed unsolvable by veteran detectives. Sterling solved the case and was moved to the police department's homicide unit.

As a homicide detective, Inspector Sterling has solved 356 of 387 homicide cases, a closure rate of 92 percent. Inspector Sterling credited his ability to close cases to being a student of human nature and being good at telling when people were lying. A major case that Inspector Sterling solved was a double murder of a husband-and-wife minister couple. The case had been unsolved for over five years. The inspector solved the case in a matter of a month. The inspector took a needed vacation at the Grand Hotel, only to be involved in a murder case there, "Inspector Sterling: The Case of the Wondering Minister."

When we last left the inspector, he had made his way back home to Chicago and was preparing to travel to Istanbul to help his friend Kevin in solving a kidnapping, a murder, and a stolen ottoman artifact. The inspector is worried about his friend Kevin Hanes and wonders about the situation that he will find once he arrives in Istanbul.

The inspector ponders: Istanbul, the former capital of the Ottoman Empire, is an enchanting place rich in history and intrigue. There are some countries in the world where the capitals and the most famous cities don't match. Istanbul is one of them. Being the most famous city of Turkey, it is no more the capital of the Turkish Republic. It is the center of everything in Turkey. History, economy, finance,trade and much more, now a kidnapping, a murder and a stolen artifact.

LIST OF CHARACTERS

Inspector Charles Anthony Sterling: A world-famous homicide detective whose best friend is Kevin Hanes. The inspector solves murders and has a high success rate. He has just finished a case in upstate New York in the Catskills.

Mustafa Muhammed: An Iraqi national. Works for the US Embassy as a translation expert in Arabic languages. Just started his job about a month ago. Previously worked as a bartender at the Grand Hotel, where Inspector Sterling got to know him and rely on him for information regarding guests who were staying at the hotel.

Dr. Reverend Sterling Halt: A noted theologian with expertise in Old and New Testament writings, especially those with Aramaic writing. Aramaic inscriptions dating from the Hellenistic and Roman periods have been discovered in regions like Cilicia, Hatay, and southeastern Turkey. The Turkish government calls upon the Dr. Reverend's expertise from time to time.

Ms. Elizabeth Jackson: A wealthy multimillionaire who has been investing in start-up product call centers in Turkey. Is one of the major investors in Kevin Hanes's start-up company in Turkey. Ms. Jackson knows what she wants and goes after it.

Kevin Hanes: A wealthy entrepreneur who has invested in a start-up company that is a call center or various products. Kevin has been in Turkey for the past three years and has built a successful company-Hao Technologies, form the ground up by recruiting local talent and promoting them into key management positions.

Mr. Jerry Davison: A former owner of the Grand Hotel with over twenty-five years' experience in hotel and restaurant management. He has just taken over the management of the Hotel Miughaamara, which is a grand hotel located in the heart of the city of Istanbul.

Reverend Michael Cramer: A former FBI agent with experience in Middle Eastern cultures. He is currently serving as an interim minister for the Unitarian Universalist Church in Los Angeles but has taken a year's sabbatical.

Ms. Nancy Donaldson: Former director of finance for the Interim Ministers Network. Just took a new career opportunity as the director of finance at the Hotel Mughaamara in Istanbul, Turkey. She has a keen since of financial management and has experience in working in foreign exchanges.

Ahmet Yilmaz: Vice president of operations for Hao Technologies, a technology company specializing in cataloging and selling ancient works of art as well as creating a platform for new and upcoming artists in the region and beyond.

Asil Ozturk: Vice president of finance for Hao Technologies and has worked for Hao Technologies for four years. Before that, worked for ORT as director of finance. Single and, in spare time, trades Ottoman Empire Collectables.

Richard Franklin: Vice president of marketing for Hao Technologies and helped to create their newest campaign centered around the artifacts on display at the National Palace's Painting Museum.

Reverend Janice Turner: A United Methodist minister and a former director of an international marketing company. Currently in Istanbul on a six-month sabbatical from her church.

Reverend Austin Roper: A United Church of Christ minister and a former peace corps worker with a background in languages.

Selim Aksu: A Turkey nationalist who is an international dealer in Ottoman artifacts and a member of the Turkey Art Ottoman Collectibles Society.

TABLE OF CONTENTS

Prologue	vii
Chapter 1: The Journey	1
Chapter 2: The Arrival	8
Chapter 3: The Mystery Continues	12
Chapter 4: The Sealed Envelope	16
Chapter 5: Hotel Miughaamara	20
Chapter 6: The Midnight Meeting	26
Chapter 7: The Lost Manuscript	33
Chapter 8: The Blue Mosque	37
Chapter 9: The Bosporus Strait	47
Chapter 10: Maiden's Tower	55
Chapter 11: Old Friends	60
Chapter 12: The Clues	67
Chapter 13: More Clues	73
Chapter 14: More Answers	78
Chapter 15: Nancy's Information	83
Chapter 16: Another Exciting Adventure	87
Chapter 17: A Conversation with Inspector Sterling	91
Chapter 18: Kevin's Confession	95
Chapter 19: The Discovery	102
Chapter 20: More Facts to Uncover	106
Chapter 21: The Plan	115
Epilogue: Let the Facts Speak	121
Photos	130
About the Author	145

CHAPTER 1

THE JOURNEY

Having just finished solving an interesting case in the Catskills of New York, I wasn't looking forward to stepping into another case of murder. When the call came from my dear friend Kevin Hanes from Istanbul, I had to respond. Kevin and I have known each other for over twenty years, and he has supported me, traveled with me, and helped me to solve several cases. He has a keen eye for details and has always been an adventurous type. Kevin and I worked together for ten years at the Chicago Police Department as homicide detectives, and I enjoyed his keen since of people and how he could tell whether they were telling you the truth.

Kevin left the Chicago Police Department three years ago to work in Turkey as a chief operating officer at a technology start-up in Istanbul. He has loved his work with Hao Technologies and was able to put together a high-powered staff of people that were Turkish nationals.

Kevin was one of those people who did a lousy job of staying in contact, but when he did contact me, I knew it was serious. After his phone call about asking me to come because of his staff disappearing and now one of them having their throat slashed, I knew he needed someone he could trust. I wasn't entirely sure what Kevin had gotten involved with, but knowing Kevin, I know it was not the everyday type of work that he was involved with.

Kevin had always been fascinated with the Ottoman Empire, in which Turkey played a key role.

The Ottomans were known for their achievements in art, science, and medicine. Istanbul and other major cities throughout the empire were recognized as artistic hubs. Some of the most popular forms of art included calligraphy, painting, poetry, textiles and carpet weaving, ceramics, and music.

Ottoman architecture also helped define the culture of the time. Elaborate mosques and public buildings were constructed during this period. Science was regarded as an important field of study. The Ottomans learned and practiced advanced mathematics, astronomy, philosophy, physics, geography, and chemistry. Additionally, some of the greatest advances in medicine were made by the Ottomans. They invented several surgical instruments that are still used today, such as forceps, catheters, scalpels, pincers, and lancets.

Kevin had made it his practice when arriving in Istanbul to begin to study the Ottoman story and found that there was a very active artistic market for the sale and trade of Ottoman artifacts. Kevin had discovered that carpets and textiles, ceramics and tiles, calligraphy, and manuscripts and Qurans all had price tags, and all were part of the collective selling and marketing of Ottoman artifacts.

I informed Kevin that I would take the next flight available from Chicago to Munich and from Munich to Istanbul. I booked my flight and hired an Uber to take me to the airport. Within less than five minutes, I received a text; my rider had arrived to take me to O'Hare airport. I was not looking forward to the eight-hour flight to Munich. Kevin had sent me some information about the types of Ottoman artifacts and all about an art show that was happening when I arrived. Knowing Kevin, I knew that he had done a lot of investigating even before he reached out to me. Kevin sent to me some encrypted files that I planned on reviewing on the plane.

I made my way to my door and took one last look at my condo. Not sure when I would see it again, but I closed and locked my door and made my way to the elevator. My condo was on the fourth floor in the corner, and I had views of both Lake Michigan and the John Hancock building. As I made my way to the elevator, I couldn't help but wonder just what adventures and experiences I would have in Istanbul. I pushed the button to call the elevator, and it quickly arrived. When the doors opened, I was greeted by a middle-aged

CHAPTER 1

man of Middle Eastern descent. He called me by name. "Inspector Sterling, how are you?" He then introduced himself as Selim Aksu and said that Kevin had contacted him and asked him if he would be my guide and assist me in my arrival in Istanbul. We exchanged glances, and then the elevator door opened, and we both made our way to the front door and out to the street, where our Uber driver was waiting.

Selim put the bags into the trunk of the car and crawled into the back seat close to me. We were soon in early morning traffic, and the driver was staying calm and negotiating the traffic lanes to get us on the right freeway out to O'Hare airport. I had driven this route many times over the years and knew it well. Selim asked me if Kevin had informed me of all that had been happening in Istanbul. I explained that Kevin had called me and told me that three of his top managers were missing and that the body of one of them, Ahmet Yilmaz, had been found in the subway downtown with his throat slit.

Selim went on to explain that Ahmet had been the curator in charge of an Ottoman art show that was currently taking place at Topkapi Palace. Topkapi Palace, an architectural marvel that celebrates the rich culture and history of the Ottoman Empire, was a great place to hold an Ottoman art show. Selim went on to say that Ahmet had chosen the palace because of its rich cultural history, and he had known its art curator, Emre Tarkan, for years, and both believed it would be a great place to showcase Ottoman art. Ahmet was excited about one special Ottoman artifact; it was called the Emerald Dagger. The Emerald Dagger was an emerald-studded, curved dagger, and it had been created by Ottoman craftsmen in 1789 as a gift to the shah of Persia. The night before the show was to open, the dagger ended up missing, and Emre was found murdered in the basement of the Topkapi Palace.

Ahmet was also missing as well as Asil Ozturk, vice president of Finance for Hao Technologies, and Richard Franklin, vice president of marketing for Hao Technologies. A few days after the robbery, Ahmet's body had been found in the Istanbul subway with his throat slit. "Kevin turned to me," Selim said, "for help, except I had to flee the country because I was considered one of the chief suspects. Kevin told me that he has sent you some files that will explain who might be behind the theft and the murder. As to a reason as to why and who committed the murder, Kevin said that you, Inspector Sterling, would figure that out because that is what you do."

Just then our driver asked, "What airline?" and I responded, "Lufthansa, please." Selim got out first and made his way to the trunk. When opened, he reached in and lifted out my bags and his small bag. I looked over and found the door, entered, and made my way to the Lufthansa counter. We still had three hours before our flight left for Munich. Selim presented his passport and what seemed like several minutes passed, but it was only a few. The agent issued Selim's boarding pass, turned to me, and asked for my passport. The agent took one glance and issued my boarding pass. We would be flying out of Gate 27. The agent, Tamera, wished us both a great flight and instructed us where to connect with TSA and security. We made our way to security, and even though I was TSA approved, we both still had a long line at security. After about ten minutes, both of us were next to be called to come up to the TSA agent. I presented my passport and was waved through. Selim did the same, but he was held up as the agent had to call over his supervisor for approval. They asked Selim several questions about long he had been in the United States and where his destination was.

Finally, he was okayed, and we both prepared to go through the next phase of the security operation: the body scan. In no time at all, we both made it through the body scan and made our way to our gate. I told Selim that we had time and that there was a great café on our way to our gate called the Berghoff Café. "The Berghoff Café is a great German café," I said to Selim, "known for its popular hot carved sandwiches, Rubens sauerkraut, and more. The bread is baked from scratch daily. The café has been a favorite of mine for years. Whenever I am traveling internationally from O'Hare, I always stop and enjoy their food."

Selim agreed to stop, and we both made our way to the café. Once seated, we were quickly presented with menus. I knew what I wanted: the turkey BLT on sourdough with jalapeño bacon, lettuce, tomato, avocado, sriracha aioli, fried jalapeños, and house chips. Selim looked over the menu and decided to go with the grilled lamb burger. It was an infused lamb patty with roasted garlic, fresh mint, and lemon, topped with feta cheese, arugula, tomato, and lemon aioli, on a house-made kaiser bun, served with sweet potato fries.

We motioned for our server, He came over and, in a friendly manner, introduced himself as Omar. He looked like an Omar: short black hair with a nicely trimmed dark beard and mustache. I was taken back by his extremely

CHAPTER 1

good looks and his wonderful smile. Omar said, "What would you like to order today?" I immediately thought, "More like you, Omar," but then my mind drifted back to the present, and I responded that I wanted a turkey BLT, and Selim responded that he would like the infused lamb patty.

We both watched as Omar quickly went to the kitchen to provide them with our orders. I was curious as to this hotel that Kevin had arranged for me to stay at. It was called the Miughaamara, which in Arabic means "adventure." According to my friend Kevin, this hotel was located right in the middle of the old town of Istanbul. I asked Selim if he had heard of it, and he responded, "The Miughaamara Hotel was originally built in 1892 to host passengers of the Orient Express. It became known as the 'oldest European hotel of Turkey.' The hotel is notable for having hosted illustrious guests from, Agatha Christie to Ernest Hemingway."

I thanked Selim and thought, "How exciting. Another old hotel to stay in. I wonder what mysteries and stories it must tell."

Just then Omar arrived with our food and asked if there was anything else we needed. I said no and thanks for the quick service. We both devoured our food and said not a word to each other. I was beginning to like this Selim and wondered just how he and Kevin had gotten connected. Speaking of Kevin, I heard the ding of my cell phone, telling me that I had received a text message. I picked it up and looked at who had sent the message. It was from Kevin; he was just checking in to see where I was on my journey and said that he had a lot to share with me and wanted to know if I had had a chance to review the files that he had sent.

I answered his text and thanked him for arranging to have Selim accompany me. Within a few minutes, Kevin texted me back and said, "I didn't arrange for Selim to accompany you; in fact, the Turkish police are looking for him because they have a warrant out for his arrest for the murder of Ahmet Yilmaz." He asked me not to tell Selim anything about our texting conversation and to just play along.

Selim had stepped away to use the restroom while I was texting with Kevin. When he came back, Selim asked me who had texted me, and I responded, "Oh, it's just my office in Chicago checking up on me." He looked at me puzzled and like he was going to say something, and then he just sat down. Omar brought our check and processed our payment. We both got up and walked to Gate 27, which we could see from the restaurant. We still had an hour before we would start boarding, so I sent a text to my office assistant, Aphrodite, to ask her to do some research and find out everything she could about Selim Aksu and to send me what she finds.

We had time to kill, and I didn't want Selim to suspect that I had found out that Kevin had never sent him to accompany me, so I decided to engage him in conversation. I asked Selim if he could tell me about the art theft that had taken place in Turkey. Selim begin by saying from 2005 through 2009, a group of criminals and museum officials were believed to have stolen a trove of artworks and antiques, up to 302 works of art, from the State Art and Sculpture Museum. The thieves replaced 46 of the stolen pieces of art with fakes. Only three individuals from the group had been arrested, and fifteen were still on the run. Some of the artworks and antiques had been recovered, but the vast majority remained unaccounted for.

Selim went on to explain that Kevin and Ahmet had worked hard over the past three years to build a strong art collector network and that his technology company, Hao Technologies, had become well known as a resource for information about artwork, especially artifacts from the Ottoman Empire. Kevin had learned about the Emerald Dagger, which was believed to have magical healing powers. Kevin, with the assistance of Ahmet, had acquired the rights to display the dagger from a well-known art curator, Emre Tarkin, who was believed to be the mastermind behind the great art thefts back in 2005 through 2009. The authorities never were able to prove that it was him, but good, reliable sources confirmed that he could have done such a thing.

Our station agent began to announce that they were ready to board our flight. They asked for frequent flyers and first class to board first. I was flying first class, and Selim was flying economy. I told Selim that I would see him at our next gate at the Munich airport for our flight to Istanbul. I found my seat quickly: Row 4, Seat B, an aisle seat. In the seat next to me was my new friend Nancy Donaldson. I was surprised to see her and asked her where her destination was. She replied that she was flying to Istanbul to start her new position as vice president of finance for the Hotel Miughaamara. She explained that after working for well over eighteen years for the Interim Ministers Network, she was contacted by an international recruiter, and she was encouraged to

CHAPTER 1

apply she applied and was hired. I explained to her that I was headed to Istanbul to work on a new case and that I would be staying at her hotel.

I thought, "Wow, Nancy was a big help to me in my last case. She is very detail oriented and a good listener. I am very happy to have her along on this adventure." Nancy and I talked about my last case, the Case of the Wondering Minister, and how amazed she was when it was revealed who was behind the murders. I told her a little about the case. "My friend and colleague Kevin Hanes is the CEO of Hao Technologies company in Istanbul that deals with the cataloging, selling, and connecting of Turkish art and Ottoman era artifacts." I explained that one of Kevin's employees had been murdered by having his throat slit and that two others of his top managers were missing and believed to have been kidnapped.

Nancy listened and told me that she had been hired to clean up the company's financials. She had been hired on a contract basis, not only at the hotel but also at Hao Technologies, for the next year with the possibility of extending if things work out. Nancy was smart and very efficient, and I could understand why Kevin would hire her. She asked me if I was aware of the Emerald Dagger and that it had been insured for millions of dollars just before it ended up missing. She also shed light on the fact that Hao Technologies was in great financial trouble going all the way back to 2009, and Ahmet Yilmaz, the man who had had his throat slit, was connected to the art thefts back in 2005 through 2009. Kevin had hired Nancy to go back and do an audit of files to see if there was any connection with the Ottoman artifact, the Emerald Dagger, that had wound up missing.

Out of the corner of my eye, I saw Selim walk by as he was headed to the back of the plane. I was happy to be seated in first class, next to Nancy, and just knew that I would have an enjoyable flight from Chicago to Munich. Munich is seven hours ahead of Chicago. It was 1:00 p.m. Chicago time. We would be landing in Munich around 4:00 a.m. It was going to be a long flight. I prepared for takeoff, and in no time, we were in the air. I turned to Nancy and said my peace, closed my eyes, and slept. Munich, here we come, and then onto Istanbul.

CHAPTER 2

THE ARRIVAL

I awoke to hearing the flight attendant ask me if I would like some coffee. I glanced over, and Nancy appeared to still be asleep. I looked at my watch, time 7:00 a.m. We would be landing in Munich in about ninety minutes. I had slept soundly for well over five hours. Just then Nancy awoke, smiled, and spoke. "Good morning, Inspector. How are you this morning?"

I responded, "Wonderful. It was going to be a great day." I could feel it in my bones, and my body was awake and ready to tackle whatever the day would bring. Nancy asked me if I wanted to hear some information that she had learned about Kevin's company. I responded, "Absolutely."

Nancy shared with me a little more that she had discovered about my friend Kevin's company. She had discovered that ever since 2009, there had been a yearly deposit of $500,000, and it was recorded as art royalties, yet it wasn't tied to any work of art. The deposits continued each December for ten years. The check was drawn on the Bank of England, and the company was listed as Art Fair. Art Fair went out of business in 2020, and their president was Ahmet Yilmaz (Kevin's vice president of Hao Technologies). Ahmet had been missing and ended up having his throat slit and his body deposited at the subway station in downtown Istanbul.

CHAPTER 2

Kevin had hired Nancy on a contract basis to use her experience in financial auditing to look over the books of his company and trace where the funds went over those ten years.

Nancy had learned that both Selim Aksu, the gentleman that had appeared outside my condo in Chicago, and Ahmet were investors in the Hotel Miughaamara, where Nancy had been hired on contract to be their interim vice president of finance. I was amazed at just how much information Nancy had found regarding the background information the people that my friend Kevin had hired. We finished our discussion just as the head flight attendant announced, "Prepare for landing." We were about to complete our first leg of our trip to Istanbul.

The plane touched down and began its slow push to our assigned gate. It was now approaching 8:00 a.m., and our flight for Istanbul wasn't until 11:45 a.m. The plane stopped; we had arrived at our gate. The flight attendants said, "Cross check," and within a few minutes, the plane door was open, and the passengers in front of us were quickly making their way out of the plane. Nancy and I were seated in Row 5, so in no time at all, she and I were making our way off the plane. I suggested that we stop and get breakfast at a great bistro named Boconero. It was known for its great brewed coffee and its excellent bakery items. We had landed in Terminal 1, and it was in Terminal 2, but our next flight on Turkish Airlines was out of Terminal 2.

We left the walkway bridge and found our way to the moving walkway. I had forgotten all about Selim, who was at the back of the plane, but I was confident that he had found his way around airports and that we would see him at our gate. While the two of us were navigating the moving walkways, Nancy informed me that her new boss at the hotel was Mr. Jerry Davison, the former owner of the Grand Hotel. He sold the Grand Hotel to wealthily multimillionaire Ms. Elizabeth Jackson, and Ms. Jackson just happened to be one of the major investors in Kevin Hanes's company, Hao Technologies. Nancy asked me if I remembered Mustafa, who had been the bartender at the Grand Hotel. I said yes; he made me my famous drink, "the Sterling," and he gave me a lot of information that really helped me to solve the case. Nancy said that much to her surprise, Mustafa had been hired by the US Embassy in Istanbul as an Arabic translator and an attaché to the Turkish ambassador. Our walkway came to an end, and I spotted the bistro up ahead and on the right. Both of us were anxious to have some good coffee and continue our discussion.

Within no time at all, we arrived at the bistro and were quickly seated at a table in the corner that looked out onto the various gates at the airport. Everywhere I looked all I could see was the famous Turkish Airways logo on plane after plane. Munich was a major hub for Turkish Airways. Our server appeared just as we were seated and asked, "What would you like to drink?"

We both replied, "Coffee, and make it black with no cream." The server, whose name was Gunther, smiled and said he would be back with the coffees and then would take our food orders.

I wanted the German pancakes, often called Dutch Baby pancakes. They are baked pancakes made from eggs, milk, flour, and vanilla. The pancakes are baked in a metal or cast-iron pan, puff up in the oven, and then fall as they cool. My Jewish grandmother use to make them for my sister and me when we were young. I always liked to watch them puff up in the oven and then fall when you took them out of the oven. Nancy ordered the schnitzel, which is a dish that the Germans are known for.

Right after we ordered, I saw, out of the corner of my eye, Selim Aksu pass us by. He had a look of being quite stressed on his face. I noticed right behind him was the airport security in pursuit. My mind shifted to what had he been involved with. Just then a shot rang out from somewhere above in the terminal. It was a direct hit, and Selim dropped to the ground. The airport security scattered but were not able to pinpoint where the fatal bullet had come from. I got up from my seat and excused myself to Nancy and quickly went to where the body was on the floor and the security guard surrounding it. I explained that I knew the gentleman and that I was a police inspector from the United States. I showed them my credentials. We were waiting for one of the several airport doctors to arrive and to check out the body. It had already been confirmed by the airport security and by me that Selim was dead.

I racked my brain to understand why this could have happened and wondered who was behind this and why. I had another murder on my plate, and I couldn't' help but think that somehow this one was connected to the other one. Both men had a connection with Kevin, my friend. Both had very rich, colorful pasts. If this was any indication of how my time was going to be spent in Istanbul, then I was in for another wild ride.

CHAPTER 3
THE MYSTERY CONTINUES

Nancy and I spent the next hour with airport security, trying to trace Selim's steps from when he got off the plane. Neither one of us had waited for him; why would we be both headed to our gate for our flight to Istanbul? We had stopped to get some breakfast and were enjoying a great discussion when I spotted Selim out of the corner of my eye, heard the shot, and watched as his body dropped to the floor. Security had no idea as to how this happened, and their security cameras picked up no spurious characters. I learned that the Turkish authorities had been called and that Selim's body would be transported back to Turkey for a memorial and burial.

In Turkish culture, dead people are buried as soon as possible. While dead people are being buried, the thirty-sixth sura (section) of Quran is recited. If the dead is a maiden or a newly married woman, a red wreath is put on top of the grave. If the dead is a young man or a soldier, the flag of the country is raised. Selim had served in the Turkish military, so I am sure that the flag of Turkey would be raised as part of his burial ceremony.

Most Turkish burials are carried out during the afternoon namaz, or prayer time. The coffin or casket is laid into the ground with the deceased person's right side aligned with the direction of Mecca. After prayers, the body is taken to the burial site in a silent procession. Some Muslim communities

CHAPTER 3

allow women and children to attend the burial, but traditionally it's just men. Another important Islamic burial rite is to have each person at the burial throw three handfuls of dirt into the grave.

I explained all of this to Nancy, who had no idea when it came to the rituals and traditions of Islam and the Turkish culture. In thinking ahead, I thought, "Perhaps the people who are responsible for Selim's murder might come to his memorial service." I had learned through the years when working on a murder case that many times, the murderer was right in plain sight the whole time. Hopefully, I silently wished that would be the case in this situation.

Several hours had passed since we landed in Munich, and now Nancy and I were walking briskly to our gate so we could board our plane to Istanbul. According to my cell phone, we still had over forty-five minutes until we would start boarding. The airport was abuzz with chatter, and many types of people from all over were walking by the two of us. I could hear the various languages been spoken, Italian, German, French, and of course, English.

As we got closer to our gate, from out of nowhere, Ms. Elizabeth Jackson appeared. Nancy remembered her from our last encounter at the Grand Hotel. Ms. Jackson was a wealthy multimillionaire who has made her fortunes through investing in real estate as well as in start-up companies. My friend Kevin, in an earlier conversation, had asked me what I knew about Ms. Jackson. I explained to him that I had found her to be very direct and the type of businesswoman who knew what she wanted and went after it. I wondered why she was in Munich, and I wondered where she was going.

The last time our paths crossed was at the Grand Hotel in Nephi, New York, and Ms. Jackson, if I remembered correctly, had been trying to purchase the old Grand Hotel from its owners Mr. Jerry Davison and his partner.

Nancy and I quickened our pace, and soon we were neck and neck with Ms. Jackson. I called her name. "How are you, Ms. Jackson?"

Elizabeth turned and noticed me instantly and said, "Inspector Sterling, what a pleasant surprise." We exchanged pleasantries, and then Ms. Jackson acknowledged Nancy and asked, "What are you doing here?"

Nancy explained that she was on her way to Istanbul to start her new Job at the Hotel Miughaamara in downtown Istanbul. "Have you heard of that hotel?" Nancy asked Ms. Jackson.

"Heard of it? I own a quarter of it. I was looking for a good investment, and when I learned that Mr. Jerry Davison, the former owner and manager of the Grand Hotel was going to be managing the property, I had to invest."

"Wow," I thought. "Isn't that something? Mr. Davison here in Istanbul and working with Ms. Jackson. That is interesting, considering their previous interaction with each other where Ms. Jackson was trying to buy out Mr. Davison's interest in the Grand Hotel. Life always has these interesting twists and turns. We just never know who is going to end up where and who will be connected to whom."

Nancy and I finally reached our gate, and of course, Ms. Jackson was on the same flight that we were to Istanbul. The flight itself would take about two hours and forty-five minutes, and then, since that airport was located outside of the city, we would have another forty-five-minute to an hour ride from the airport into the city center of Istanbul, where our hotel was located. I was hoping to meet my friend Kevin at 7:30 p.m. in the lobby of the hotel that evening. Just then, the flight attendant announced that Flight 2789 would begin boarding for Istanbul. She referenced premier members and anyone traveling with children first, then those in the 1 boarding group, which included Nancy, myself, and Ms. Jackson. The three of us made our may to the flight attendant and checked in and began the walk to the door of the plane. Because we were all in first class, we took another route to the plane in boarding that the others didn't have access to.

The three of us boarded the plane and found our way quickly to our assigned seats. Nancy and I were seated in Row 4, Seats 3 and 4, and apparently Ms. Jackson was in Row 2, seat 3, which was the first set of seats when you entered the airplane. While we were waiting for the plane to take off, our flight attendant, Jack, brought us some drinks and some finger foods. I settled into my seat and anxiously waited for the plane to take off. Nancy and I were pretty much all talked out, and Ms. Jackson was too far away, so I was hoping that I could do some writing in my case book to jot down all that I knew so far about this case.

I couldn't help but think that it was strange that Selim appeared at my condo and that Kevin had not sent him. Also, that for some reason, he had been shot by a sniper at the Munich airport. What was Selim's connection to the Emerald Dagger and to the Ottoman artifact art show? Why did the Turkish

CHAPTER 3

police want him arrested, and why did he leave Turkey to fly to Chicago to meet me? I wonder if he was trying to tell me something about the case but never had the opportunity to speak about it. He kept talking about the files that Kevin had sent me. Perhaps there were some sorts of clues in those files. All of this was one big mystery with a lot of unanswered questions. Two murders, one missing artifact, and a wild tale about a Turkish art theft. I certainly had my work cut out for me and a lot of pieces to tie together. I was more than enthusiastic to arrive in Istanbul so I could begin to unravel and learn about this case. Just then I heard the pilot welcome us and announce to the crew to prepare the plane for takeoff. We slowly pulled away from our gate and made our way onto the tarmac and eventually onto Runway 909. We started to accelerate down the runway and soon we were airborne. It was time for me to rest and to ponder the mystery that was unfolding for me.

CHAPTER 4
THE SEALED ENVELOPE

Nancy sat quietly in her seat as if to take in all that had occurred. I, on the other hand, couldn't help but review in my mind the past day's events. The murder of Selim Aksu at the Munich airport, the slashing of Ahmet Yilmaz throat in Istanbul before we arrived, and the knowledge that Kevin had not arranged for Selim to come to Chicago and to escort me to Istanbul. Questions about these murders began to form in my mind. What did Selim know, and why would someone want to have him killed? If he was part of the original art theft back in 2008 through 2011, what happened to the art, and why were many copies made and then sold as originals? Where were the paintings? Were they still out there? What did all of this have to do with Kevin's company and the art show about the Ottoman artifacts, and particularly the Emerald Dagger?

Nancy was in a bit of a panic in one way. She had taken a new position at the hotel and, at the same time, had agreed to look over Kevin's finances for his company and perform an internal audit. Where was the famous Emerald Dagger, and where were the missing employees being held? Nancy offered to me in strict confidence her uneasiness, given the current situation of what had occurred. I assured her that I would have her back and that we would solve this case.

CHAPTER 4

For the next hour, we both sat there in silence. I went over in my mind as best as I could all the events that had occurred over the past several hours. Selim had appeared outside my door and said that Kevin had sent him, only for me to find out later that Selim was being held for murder in Istanbul for the murder of Emre Tarkin, the director of the art show who had been the curator who obtained the right to display the Emerald Dagger. Emre was also believed to be the mastermind behind the art thefts from 2005 through 2009. Selim knew about the art theft ring as well as the theft of the dagger. Why would they kill Selim in such a public place? Was it a message to me?

I was looking forward to meeting Kevin and questioning him and going over all the files that he had collected regarding Selim, the art theft, and his own company. Kevin still had two others top managers in his company that were missing and no contact from the kidnappers. My case right now was to do all that I could to get the employees back and in one piece. The murder of Selim and Kevin's manager had to be solved as well, but I wasn't sure if they were connected.

The flight attendant asked if I would like something to drink, and of course, I said, "Yes, bring me a vodka tonic." She returned with the necessary ingredients, and I took the time to mix them all together. It was awesome. I would have offered Nancy something, but she appeared to be fast asleep. The drink calmed my nerves and provided me clarity in my mind. Somehow the art theft ring in 2008 and the murder of the art curator and the theft of the emerald dagger had to be connected, as well as the killing of Selim at the Munich airport.

Kevin had invited me in to help him get his kidnapped employees back. I hadn't counted on Ottoman artifacts, a killing in front of my own eyes at the Munich airport, and a famous Ottoman artifact winding up missing and possibly stolen. Kevin had a lot of explaining to do. Just then I heard over the plane speaker, "We will be starting our approach to the Istanbul airport." Yes, we would finally be on the ground in about twenty minutes. I was ready for this Istanbul adventure to begin.

Nancy appeared to be awake and smiled and asked if we were close to landing. I replied, "Yes, in about twenty minutes."

Nancy uttered, "Thank God." The flight attendants made their way through the cabin, picking up any trash. Unbeknownst to me the flight attendant discovered in the airplane bathroom a small package that was addressed to Inspector Sterling, first class. The flight attendant brought it to the attention of the main attendant in charge, and they called security. There appeared to be something wrapped inside. They were instructed to carefully unwrap the package, in which there appeared to be a jeweled knife with a small, sealed envelope around it that read, "Deliver to Inspector Sterling in first class." The head flight attendant asked if I and my companion could stay on the plane and be the last to leave, as she had something important to share with us.

The plane landed in Istanbul, and I heard the same flight attendant proclaim, "Welcome to Istanbul. Please remain in your seats with the seat belt fastened until we come to a complete stop at the gate." The plane slowly made its way to the gate, and the captain turned off the seat-belt light, and passengers began to freely move about the cabin. Nancy and I remained in our seats and watched as each passenger filed by us. We had no idea what was coming our way. As the passengers filed by, I noticed someone that looked familiar but couldn't quite place the face.

Nancy missed seeing them, or I would have asked her. When all the passengers had exited, Jeanie, the head flight attendant, brought the package to us both and explained that it had been found in the bathroom at the back of the plane. The package had been unwrapped to make sure that it wasn't a bomb, and inside was this dagger. On the dagger was a small, sealed envelope addressed to Inspector Sterling. I opened the small, sealed envelope, and inside I found a card with the following written in neat handwriting: "Inspector, I know who has the kidnapped employees and where the Emerald Dagger can be found. Meet me at Hotel Miughaamara tonight at midnight and bring your friend Nancy. Tell no one, or there will be dire consequences."

The security forces already knew about the package, and they would soon learn about the note. I had been looking forward to being in Istanbul and trying to learn more from Kevin and hopefully begin to put this mystery together. Nancy, whether she liked it or not, was very much involved with trying to assist me in solving this mystery. It was clear to me that Nancy and I had been watched and by whom and why. Also, someone who was a passenger on the plane ether was directly involved or had been hired to deliver the package, but why? In all my years as a homicide detective, I'd never encountered such

CHAPTER 4

mystery and intrigue at the beginning of a case. The clues just kept dropping, but yet, I hadn't been able to connect them together.

Nancy and I made our way down the jetway and into the Istanbul terminal. We would retrieve our luggage and then be off to the hotel. When we got to our baggage claim to gather our bags, I noticed a Middle Eastern man holding a sign. It read, "Inspector Sterling and Nancy Donaldson." He approached us in broken English and explained that he had been sent to pick us up. I asked him if Kevin had hired him, and he said no, a Ms. Elizabeth Jackson had hired him. I remembered that when I saw her at the airport in Chicago, she had informed me that she had a 25 percent interest in an Istanbul hotel. This adventure was getting more and more interesting.

CHAPTER 5

HOTEL MIUGHAAMARA

Nancy and I retrieved our luggage and quickly followed our driver, whose name was Akeem. Akeem had parked his auto in a proximity to the terminal, and in no time, Nancy and I arrived at his auto. His car was a black BMW X3. Akeem opened his back of his Black BMW SUV. He picked up our luggage and directed both of us to the back seat. Nancy climbed in and slid across and situated herself right behind the driver's seat. I got in quickly. Akeem got in and started the car, and we were off. Neither Nancy nor I needed to tell Akeem where we needed to go; he sped off in the direction of the Hotel Miughaamara, Nancy's new place of work and my place of stay while in Istanbul.

Akeem asked us if we both knew anything about the Hotel Miughaamara. Akeem, before ether of us could answer, started to tell us about the hotel. Akeem stated, "Hotel Miughaamara was originally built in 1892 to host passengers of the Orient Express." (The Orient Express is arguably the most famous train line in the Western world, operating for over eighty years from 1883 to 1977, and passengers could travel from Paris to Istanbul). Akeem went on to say that the Hotel Miughaamara was known as one of the oldest hotels in Turkey; it was built between 1892 and 1895 by the architect Alexander Vallaury. He designed the hotel to have an exceptional neoclassical exterior facade and oriental interior ballroom. The hotel was the first in

CHAPTER 5

Istanbul to have electricity and hot running water, then became the first hotel in Constantinople to have an electric lift.

As for the design and decoration of the hotel, the architect wanted guests to feel like a member of the Ottoman royal family, so he based the design of the rooms on the luxury and elegance of the Ottoman palaces. Each room was named after one of the most prominent sultan's wives of the Ottoman Empire.

The hotel was known for having hosted eclectic characters such as Agatha Christie, whose favorite room was 411 and now bore her name. It was believed that this was the room where she wrote her novel *Murder on the Orient Express*. The hotel today still represented the very best in luxury and was a popular place to stay for a range of guests from Ernest Hemingway to Alfred Hitchcock.

Today the hotel has lasted through the collapse of the Ottoman Empire, two World Wars, and the establishment of the new Republic of Turkey. The hotel has been welcoming its guests in this beautiful neighborhood in the heart of Istanbul. The hotel, once called Little Europe, with its charming ambiance and luxury facilities, has gotten the attention of people for more than a century.

Akeem could have easily been a tour guide in the way he informed Nancy and me all about the hotel and its history. On our way to the city and the hotel, I asked Akeem about the Blue Mosque. Akeem gladly started in and said, "The Blue Mosque in Istanbul, also known by its official name, the Sultan Ahmed Mosque is an Ottoman-era historical imperial mosque. It was constructed between 1609 and 1617 and remains a functioning mosque today. He said that both of us needed to make the time to go on a tour to see the Blue Mosque for ourselves.

We rounded a corner, and here up to the right side stood this Gothic-looking structure that looked like it came out of another century. I quickly learned from Akeem that what I was looking at was the Hotel Miughaamara. In Arabic the name of the hotel means "adventure."

I was excited to finally be in the city of Istanbul. I knew from my historical studies that the city of Istanbul had one of the richest histories in the world and that our hotel was located right in the middle of the old town, the part of the city that had witnessed all its phases through the course of history. Many of the emperors lived around the historical peninsula of Istanbul, and many empires were governed there. These streets had hosted people from all around the world for nearly twenty-seven hundred years. The historical background of the various cultures that existed in Istanbul made it inevitable that this city would retain a different aspect of every civilization it hosted.

Akeem pulled in front of the grand old hotel. I looked up and felt as if I were experiencing history. I was looking at a building where many Ottoman leaders had lived and called home. The hotel, several years ago, had undergone an extensive renovation, and it showed with such a degree of grandeur that it took my breath away. As I was amazed at the spectacular-looking building, I heard a voice calling out my name. "Inspector Sterling, over here." I turned my gaze in the direction of the voice, and there was Kevin Hanes, my dear friend. Kevin quickly made his way over to us. I quickly took the moment to introduce Nancy and explained that she was the new vice president of finance who had just been hired on a contract basis to manage the financial status of this grand old hotel. Kevin reminded me that he also had hired Nancy to audit his company's records for the past ten years.

Kevin explained that he had arranged for the two of us—and, of course, Nancy if she wanted to—to come to join the new manager of the hotel, Mr. Jerry Davison, for dinner in the hotel restaurant, called Amanos. Kevin said, "Inspector, you will love this restaurant. They have a rooftop bar that provides one with magnificent views of the old city of Istanbul. One can see the Blue Mosque, Topkapi Palace, and the traffic on the Bosporus Strait, a well-known waterway in Istanbul." Nancy and I followed Kevin into the hotel, and Akeem was right behind with our luggage.

I was too involved with thinking about the note I had received on the plane. When we entered the lobby of the hotel, I gasped. Nancy grabbed my arm and told me to look around. As I looked around the lobby, I was greeted by a grand space adorned with elegant furnishings, intricate details, and a sense of old-world charm. I was amazed at how the architecture of the lobby reflected the hotel's rich heritage. There were ornate columns, marble floors, and intricate moldings. Large chandeliers hung from the ceiling, and they cast a warm glow over the space and added a degree of ambiance and sophistication. I noticed that comfortable seating areas were scattered throughout, inviting guests to relax and unwind. Overall, the lobby of the hotel exuded

CHAPTER 5

an elegance and grandeur, setting the tone for a memorable stay in one of Istanbul's most iconic establishments.

Kevin was leading Nancy and me across the lobby to the main check-in area, I heard a familiar voice call out, "Inspector Sterling, welcome to our hotel." I looked up and noticed that the voice was that of Mr. Jerry Davison. Mr. Davison had been the owner and manager of the Grand Hotel back in Nephi, New York, and I had gotten to know him and his business partner very well. I had learned that after I solved the case, he sold his interest in the hotel and invested in the Hotel Miughaamara and was hired on as the general manager. Jerry welcomed both Nancy and me as if we were old friends. I suppose we were, considering all that we had been put through in helping Jerry to solve who was committing the murders at his hotel. Jerry, in his usual hospitable way, immediately made me feel welcome and happy that we had chosen this hotel to stay at.

Jerry appeared not to be aware that Nancy had come to work at the hotel. Nancy mentioned that she was excited to be hired as a contract basis to be the acting vice president of finance. Jerry seemed to be not aware of her hiring, which seemed odd since he was the general manager of the hotel. Kevin turned to Jerry and asked him if he could join us for dinner later that evening. Jerry indicated that he would have to see he had another meeting scheduled but could possibly drop by and share dessert with the three of us. I watched as Jerry made his way across the lobby and out the main doors of the hotel.

Nancy said she was tired and that she would meet both of us in the lobby at seven o'clock for dinner. Finally, I had some alone time with Kevin. I suggested that we go have a drink at the bar and get all caught up on what had been happening. Keven nodded his head in approval, and off the two of us went to the hotel bar.

Nestled within the historic walls of the hotel, there was a hidden gem of a bar ensconced in one of the city's oldest hotels. As we stepped through the intricately carved wooden doors, it felt as if we were being transported to another era, where the opulence of the Ottoman Empire mingled with the modern allure of a cosmopolitan city.

The bar was adorned with rich, dark wood paneling, exuding an old-world charm that harkened us both back to a bygone era. Ornate Turkish lanterns cast a warm, inviting glow, illuminating the plush velvet upholstery of the antique furniture. Persian rugs lined the floor, adding a touch of luxury underfoot. The air was heavy with the scent of exotic spices and the heady aroma of freshly brewed Turkish coffee.

Behind the bar were shelves that seemed to groan under the weight of gleaming bottles, showcasing a vast array of spirits from around the world. A skilled bartender stood ready to concoct any libation my heart desired.

Kevin and I made our way to the closest available seats at the bar and were met by Burak, the bartender at the bar. I had remembered from my limited studies in Arabic that Burak means "to kneel down to bless." I thought it was only fitting that we had a bartender whose name meant "to bless." Considering all that was going on in both of our lives, we could use a blessing.

I ordered my usual drink, a Sterling, and Kevin ordered a dry martini. Within no time at all, Burak brought us our drinks and set them in front of us. As I sat there sipping my drink, I couldn't help but be captivated by the lively chatter that was filling the room. As I looked around, it appeared that there were travelers from far and wide mingling with locals, swapping stories and sharing laughter. I loved the ambiance, lively yet intimate. I thought this was the perfect spot for both quiet contemplation and spirited revelry.

I turned to Kevin and asked him for an update on his missing staff. He had received nothing, but a cryptic message texted to him that all would be revealed in the next seventy-two hours. Kevin had received the text message an hour before Nancy, and I had arrived in Istanbul. I looked at Kevin and asked him for some direct, honest answers. After preparing to leave Chicago and traveling here to Istanbul, I explained to him that it had been a wild drive. I asked him directly if he had sent Selim to greet me at my building when I was preparing to leave. Kevin responded that he had not sent him and was saddened to learn of his killing at the Munich airport.

Kevin shared that he had discovered that the company that he was CEO for in the past had invested money into purchasing the fake paintings that Selim was involved with marketing and selling. Kevin had discovered that Selim had created another set of books and had been hiding the investments and the money that he was sealing from the company. "I hired Nancy to do a complete audit for the past five years and to try and trace whatever individuals might have been involved in the scheme."

CHAPTER 5

I shared with Kevin about the strange package that I had received on the plane and that I was planning on meeting whoever was behind it this evening at midnight on the rooftop of the hotel. Kevin was concerned for my safety but also knew that nothing was going to stop me from meeting whoever on the hotel rooftop. I looked up at Kevin, then I glanced outside.

Outside, through the arched windows, the twinkling lights of Istanbul's skyline beckoned, casting a magical spell over the ancient city. In this timeless oasis, where history and modernity intertwined, I was reminded of the enduring allure of Istanbul and the countless tales it had yet to tell.

CHAPTER 6
THE MIDNIGHT MEETING

The allure of the city, Kevin responded, had kept him staying and working in Istanbul. "There is something magical about the city, this hotel, and the history of the Ottoman Empire that I find fascinating," Kevin stated. I had only been in the city for a few hours but felt that same allure and fascination.

Kevin went on to say, "Istanbul, formerly known as Constantinople, has a rich history that spans thousands of years, making it one of the most fascinating cities in the world. Its significance is deeply intertwined with the Ottoman Empire because Istanbul served as the capital of the Ottoman Empire for over four hundred years, from 1453 to 1922." Kevin felt that he needed to give me a bit of a history lesson in hopes that it would shed light and understanding on the present situation and the case that I was trying to solve.

Kevin turned to me and asked, "Is it OK with you that I offer to you a bit of history? Some I have discovered on my ow, but others I have been told by some of the longtime residents." I continued to look at Kevin, and he launched into this historical and cultural narrative. Kevin stated that Istanbul was the capital of two of the most significant empires in history: the Byzantine Empire and the Ottoman Empire. As such, it had been a center of political, cultural, and economic power for centuries.

Kevin went on to say, "Istanbul I believe is home to a wealth of architectural marvels from both the Byzantine and Ottoman periods. Iconic landmarks such as the Hagia Sophia, Topkapi Palace, Blue Mosque, showcase the grandeur and splendor of these empires. Istanbul's unique position as a bridge between Europe and Asia has resulted in a diverse and vibrant cultural scene. It has been influenced by various civilizations, including Greek, Roman, Byzantine, Ottoman, and modern Turkish cultures, making it a melting pot of traditions, languages, and cuisines." I listened with awe and wonder as Kevin went onto explain more.

Kevin continued, "Situated at the crossroads of Europe and Asia, Istanbul has always been a crucial hub for trade, commerce, and diplomacy. Its strategic location on the Bosporus Strait made it a prized possession for empires throughout history. The Ottoman Empire left a legacy on Istanbul and the broader region. Its administrative structures, legal systems, and cultural traditions have shaped modern-day Turkey and its neighboring countries."

I reflected on what I have learned about Istanbul, "Istanbul's rich cultural heritage is reflected in its art, literature, music, and cuisine. The city's bazaars, such as the Grand Bazaar and the Spice Bazaar, offer a glimpse into its vibrant marketplace culture, which has remained largely unchanged for centuries. As the capital of one of the most powerful empires in history, Istanbul played a significant role in shaping global politics, trade routes, and diplomatic relations. Its influence extended far beyond its borders, reaching Europe, Asia, and Africa."

Kevin stated, "Overall, the allure of Istanbul and the Ottoman Empire lies in their captivating history, breathtaking architecture, cultural diversity, and enduring legacy that continue to fascinate people around the world. This is why," Kevin loudly exclaimed, "the Emerald Dagger is an Ottoman Empire artifact that has great cultural meaning and historical significance. It is an emerald-studded, curved dagger and it was created by Ottoman craftsman in 1789 as a gift to the Shah of Persia. Kevin went on to say that the dagger has been attributed to having special powers." "In the realm of mysticism and folklore, the Emerald Dagger was believed to possess various mystical powers, such as spells or enchantments, to either curse enemies or protect the wielder. These could range from simple charms to ward off evil spirits to more elaborate rituals believed to provide invulnerability or strength. In addition, this dagger was associated with the ability to predict the future or communicate with spirits."

I sat there, listening to Kevin talk about the Emerald Dagger, and I was beginning to understand why someone might want to have it in their possession. The question in the forefront of my mind was, "Would someone be willing to kill in order to gain possession of the dagger?" For the next few minutes, Kevin and I sat in silence as we both pondered over what had transpired in this case so far: two murders; a missing, well-known Ottoman artifact; along with several manuscripts that were thought to contain writings from the prophet Mohamed.

Not to mention that three of Kevin's management team had been kidnapped, one had his throat slit, and the other two were still missing. Lots of unanswered questions and lots of possible guilty players in this twisted tale of intrigue and theft. It was time to ask Kevin the difficult questions.

"Kevin," I said, "I need you to tell me everything that you know and everything that you have found out and those things that you are wondering about. Kevin, let's start with what brought you to Istanbul and who recruited you to come and work here."

Kevin shared that he had always had a fascination with Ottoman history and had been a study of manuscripts. Kevin stated that Dr. Reverend Sterling Halt had contacted him about a year ago and wanted him to be a part of a company that specialized in cataloging and selling ancient works of art as well as creating a platform for sharing and preserving ancient manuscripts from the Byzantine and Ottoman Empires.

Kevin went on to explain that Ahmet Yilmaz and Selim Aksu had contacted Kevin about the possibility of buying and selling of ancient manuscripts, especially those that were done using Naskh and Thuluth, two prominent scripts in Islamic calligraphy, each with its distinctive characteristics and applications. "Manuscripts written in Naskh and Thuluth scripts covered a wide range of subjects, including religious texts, poetry, literature, historical documents, and official decrees," Kevin stated.

Kevin had reached out to Mustafa Mohamed, a friend of mine who was working at the US embassy in Istanbul as a translation expert in Arabic languages, especially Naskh and Thuluth scripts. Mustafa had told Kevin that many copies of the Quran were written in Naskh script due to its clarity and legibility. These manuscripts often featured elaborate ornamentation, including illuminated borders and chapter headings. Mustafa also let Kevin know

CHAPTER 6

that Thuluth script was commonly used for monumental inscriptions on mosques, madrasas, and other architectural structures. "Thuluth script lent an air of grandeur and formality to official decrees, royal edicts, and imperial orders issued by the Ottoman sultans and other Islamic rulers," Mustafa said.

Thuluth script was widely admired for its graceful curves and elongated proportions, making it a popular choice for decorative panels and calligraphic artworks. Thuluth script also adorned ceremonial objects, such as swords, shields, and seals, adding an element of prestige and significance to these items.

Kevin learned from the locals that Selim Aksu had been involved with an art theft ring, and Ahmet Yilmaz had both been part of a crime syndicate that stole up to 302 works of art from 2005 to 2009. This group of criminals was believed to have stolen the trove of artworks and antiques from the State Art and Sculpture Museum. An anonymous caller cracked open the organized crime syndicate. The anonymous caller, said to be an antiques dealer himself and referred to by the pseudonym "Daylight," revealed that Ahmet Yilmaz, the group's leader, had helped the gang to earn approximately $250 million through the sale and forgery of famous artworks. Kevin had learned that three individuals from the group were arrested, but fifteen were still on the run.

According to "Daylight," after the originals were removed from the museum, the group "sold them to famous businessmen through mediators and antique dealers known in their fields." The source claims to have been approached by Asel Ozturk, vice president of Hao Technologies, presumably to participate in the scheme, and that he was later threatened with death if he exposed the organization's activities.

Kevin went onto say that several of the stolen works had been recovered, but the vast majority remained unaccounted for. I thanked Kevin for all the information that he had shared with me. Not only was I coming into murders, but also art thefts, manuscripts, and forgeries, and somehow, they all had to be related. Perhaps at midnight tonight, I would learn from the mysterious caller that I was to be meeting. I asked Kevin if he wanted to join me, but he declined, given that he had to be up early to catch a plane to Munich, Germany.

I looked at my watch: 10:00 p.m. Two more hours before I would make my way to the top floor of the hotel and meet this mysterious person on the roof deck. Several thoughts raced through my mind. I realized that Kevin had reached out to me because of the complexity of this case and the need to see where everything was connected. Much to my surprise, I looked over, and sitting on the far table in the bar was none other than my friend Mustafa Mohamed, who saw me and motioned for me to come over and join the people at his table.

I quickly made my way across the room, and lo and behold, there was Ms. Elizabeth Jackson, the wealthy millionaire that I had met on my past case, along with Dr. Reverend Sterling Halt, the noted theologian and expert on Aramaic manuscripts, and the Reverend Michael Cramer, who was on sabbatical from his Unitarian Universalist church in Los Angeles. I remembered that I had met Michael as well in my last case at the Grand Hotel. What I had remembered about Michael was that he had been an FBI agent who had extensive experience with Middle Eastern cultures.

Mustafa looked at the group gathered and, in his own unique way, stated "I believe all of you know Inspector Sterling."

They all smiled and nodded, and Ms. Jackson piped up and said, "What are you doing here, Inspector?"

That was quickly followed by Dr. Reverend Sterling Halt saying, "Yes, why are you here?"

I looked around the table and stated, "I am here on an unusual case of murder and intrigue that may involve all of you."

All at once the mood around the table went very quiet, but that was quickly changed by Mustafa saying, "Why, Inspector, how can all of us assist you?"

I explained that I would be contacting each of them just to chat and to pick their brains for ideas and for suggestions on solving this new case. A brief sigh went over the table as everyone relaxed, and they figured that I wasn't there to accuse any of them of murder.

Quickly various conversations started occurring around the table, and I found myself sitting next to Reverend Michael Cramer and asking him about how his sabbatical from his congregation was going. The reverend responded that he was enjoying being back in Istanbul and reconnecting with many of his old friends and colleagues that he had worked with when he was an FBI agent.

CHAPTER 6

I asked him if he had heard about the art theft or if he knew anything about it. He smiled and said, "That was the last case that I worked on before I left the FBI." I somehow got the impression that Reverend Michael knew more about the theft than what he was saying. I filed away in my mind that there was more there that I would need to explore at another time.

I took a glance at my watch. It was now eleven thirty, and I excused myself from the table and said that I was going to meet someone up on the roof deck and was wondering if anyone at the table wanted to join me. They all responded that they needed to be going soon but perhaps another time. I thanked them and made my way across the room and out the bar to the elevators. The elevators opened, and I pushed the button that read, "RD." The elevator rose quickly and stopped, and doors opened onto what appeared to be a terrace.

Out of the corner of my eye, I watched a young man approach me. He said, "Inspector Sterling, your party has not arrived, but they asked that I seat you in the far table in the corner." I followed the young man, and he brought me to the table. I sat down, and from where I sat, I had a great view of the roof deck. Not a whole lot of people. I wondered just whom I would be meeting with and what information they would share with me.

A glance at my watch told me that whoever it was still had five more minutes before they would be late. I looked over at the elevator, and I thought my eyes were playing tricks on me. It was Nancy Donaldson who was making her way across the room to my table. "What?" I thought. "Why would she be coming to meet with me? Could it be?"

Nancy quickly pulled out her chair and begin to sit down and at the same time said, "I can explain."

When Nancy was working for the Interim Ministers Network as the director of finance, she had gotten to know Dr. Reverend Sterling Halt and Reverend Michael Cramer. They shared with her all about the art thefts in Istanbul and about the fact that many of the works had still not been recovered, as well as that fifteen of the people involved in the art theft ring were still unaccounted for. Nancy went on to say that she had been contacted by Ms. Jackson, and she offered her a contract job at the hotel to be the acting vice president of finance. Ms. Jackson shared that she knew the informer known

31

as "Daylight." She explained that she knew who the mastermind behind the art thefts were and recently who had stolen the Emerald Dagger.

"She had asked me to find a way to get you to take this case and to meet with her. When she saw you earlier in the evening, she contacted me and asked if I could meet with you and explain. She said that she had something to take care of but would meet you in the morning and explain everything. She indicated that the missing employees of Kevin were being held at the Blue Mosque and that when you find them, you will find the missing Emerald Dagger." Nancy thanked me for coming and indicated that she had to leave. She left, and I watched her walk across the room and get into the elevator. I sat there in silence and still not completely clear as to what was going on.

After what seemed like a long span of time but was most likely only about five minutes, I motioned for the young man to come over and asked him for my bill. He said, "Oh, it's on the house, compliments of Mr. Jerry Davison, the general manager."

"How odd," I thought. I hadn't told him about my meeting. I waited for the elevator, and it seemed to be stopped on the fifth floor. Finally, it made its way up and opened. There, in the corner of the elevator, with a dagger in her heart was Ms. Nancy Donaldson.

I called for help and waited for help to arrive. My mind started racing through all the events of this day and trying to find connections and reasons for all the meetings. Here was another murder. The only reason that I could imagine was because she had learned of who was behind the art thefts and the theft of the Emerald Dagger. I called Kevin and asked him to meet me on the roof deck.

CHAPTER 7
THE LOST MANUSCRIPT

I sat there on the roof deck, waiting for Kevin to arrive. I went over the events of the last few hours and could not understand why Nancy was killed. As far as I could remember from the conversations that Nancy and I had had on the plane, and even here at the hotel, Nancy seemed to be playing the role of being the messenger. Perhaps Ms. Elizabeth Jackson had been targeted, and killing Nancy sent a strong message that whoever was doing this meant business.

Just then the elevator rang, and out walked Kevin. The look on his face was one of stress, worry, and deep concern. Kevin quickly made his way over to where I was sitting. He yelled out, almost like a whimper, "I can't believe it. Who is behind this, and why would they want to kill Nancy?" I explained to Kevin that Nancy had told me that Kevin's missing employees along with the Emerald Dagger could be found at the Blue Mosque.

The paramedics arrived and confirmed that death was brought about by a stab to the heart. Nancy died instantly and did not have to suffer long. The weapon was a pearl-encrusted dagger like the one that had gone missing from the art show. It was important to note that a dagger is a fighting knife with a very sharp point and usually one or two sharp edges, typically designed to be or capable of being used as a cutting or thrusting weapon.

A dagger's blade's tang extends through the handle, which is cylindrical, normally carved from wood or bone. In cross section, the blade is usually diamond shaped, lenticular, or triangular. These blades have a sharpened point. The forensic doctor who examined the murder indicated that both the edges of the dagger were sharpened.

This dagger belonged to a large group of flamboyant, gem-studded weapons that were probably made in Istanbul in the waning years of the Ottoman Empire. Their traditional shapes and luxurious materials were intended to evoke romantic notions of the exotic Orient, Arabian Nights, or perhaps the sultan's treasury.

The questions that both Kevin and I had were, "Who would have access to these types of weapons today? And why it was used on Nancy—who, as far as Kevin and I knew, had nothing to do with any of the history of the art thefts and the history of the Ottoman Empire here in Istanbul?" Many questions raced through my head as I sat there listening and conversing with Kevin.

"What does Ms. Elizabeth Jackson have to do with all this since, according to Nancy, she was the person in the art thefts who was identified as Daylight? Also why is Reverend Cramer here at the hotel. I know he is on a year's sabbatical from his duties at the Unitarian Church of Los Angeles, but why Istanbul?" I did recall that he was a former FBI agent who had a lot of experience with Middle Eastern cultures, and Kevin told me that he had reached out to him to learn more about the art thefts.

Then there was the Dr. Reverend Sterling Halt, whom I had crossed path with before when I was working on the case that I called "The Wondering Minster." He was an expert on Aramaic writings, and from time to time, the Turkish government has hired him as a consultant to decipher manuscripts that were written in Arabic. According to Kevin, he was brought in by Ms. Jackson to aid in some manuscripts that she had come across and were up for sale.

Finally, just what did Mr. Jerry Davison know about all of this? He was the general manager of the hotel, and somehow, he had found out about my meeting because he picked up the tab for the evening. He was coming off a challenging situation at the Grand Hotel, which he recently sold to an outside investor. He was a very precise and shrewd businessman, and I did believe he would stop at nothing if he could make money from it.

CHAPTER 7

Then there was Kevin's start-up company and the work that it did in cataloging and selling ancient works of art, as well as creating a platform for new and upcoming artists in the region. Ahmet, one of Kevin's employees, was kidnapped and then murdered, and it was believed that he was involved with the art theft and the masterpiece forgery scandal, in which many of the stolen pieces had forgery copies made and then were resold as originals.

Why were the two other employees, Asel Ozturk and Richard Franklin, still being held and why hadn't there been any demands placed on their release by the kidnappers? Very strange situation, and none of it made a lot of sense. I could see some connections, but there appeared not to be anything major that connected all these individuals and the stolen art and artifacts.

What was my old friend Mustafa doing here? I knew he was working as an interpreter for the US embassy, but he said that he was reviewing some ancient Arabic manuscripts and that both Kevin and Mr. Davison had contacted him and asked for his assistance. Lots of questions, and with each question, I came up with more questions.

I turned to Kevin and said, "We need to go to the Blue Mosque and see where we can find the Emerald Dagger and your two employees. I suggest that it is now almost 2:00 a.m. Let's get some sleep and meet in the morning at nine o'clock in the lobby of the hotel." I asked Kevin if he could reach out to Ms. Jackson, Mustafa, Dr. Halt, and Reverend Cramer to join us on our adventure. He indicated that he would. I left Kevin and walked across to the elevator, pushed the button, and waited for it to arrive.

The elevator arrived within minutes. The doors opened, and I made my way in and pushed the fourth-floor button. I was on my way back to my room to get some much-needed rest. The elevator arrived on the fourth floor, and the door opened. I walked out and ran into Mustafa. He had been looking for me. Ms. Jackson had acquired an ancient Arabic manuscript that she believed was part of the "Hadith," which is a record of the sayings and deeds of the prophet Muhammed. Mustafa told me that he had begun to translate the manuscript, and it spoke of the Emerald Dagger, the one Ottoman artifact that was still missing. This manuscript would authenticate the Emerald Dagger and shed light on its origin.

I shared with Mustafa what had happened with Nancy and how she had told me that the missing employees from Kevin's company were being housed at the Blue Mosque, along with the missing Emerald Dagger. I asked him if he would join us and said that a group of us would be walking to the Blue Mosque in the morning. He said he would try and make it.

I said my goodbyes to Mustafa, and off I went to my hotel room. I opened my door and waked in, and on the floor was a brown manila envelope. I opened the envelope, and in what appeared to be a series of cut-out letters was a message. The message read, "Be careful, Inspector. Those who chase the dagger will be brought down." I looked to see if there was any sign on the envelope as it its origin. No such luck. The strange message just added more confusion to the mix and more persons to interview and rule out.

The clock by my bedside read 3:00 a.m. I quickly undressed and crawled into bed. Sleep came quickly. Before long, it was morning, and I woke to the pounding on my door and the sound of "Inspector Sterling, are you there?"

CHAPTER 8
THE BLUE MOSQUE

I looked at the clock by the beside in my room. It was 7:30 a.m. The pounding at the door continued, and I heard again the calling out of my name. "Inspector Sterling. Hello? Are you there?" I quickly made my way to the door and opened it. Much to my great surprise, it was the Reverend Michael Cramer. The reverend asked if he could come in, and he pushed his way into my room before I could answer him. He said, "Inspector, I believe I can help you."

A puzzled look came across my face. I thought, "How?" The reverend went on to say that when he worked for the FBI, he had been the agent in charge of investigating the major art thefts and had been able to obtain a quick education when it came to Middle Eastern culture, and especially art and artifacts from the Ottoman Empire.

The reverend had discovered an art/history theft ring that dealt in the trading and selling of ancient manuscripts and art from the Ottoman Empire. The Ottoman manuscripts that were being traded included texts on Islamic and Christian theology, astronomy and astrology, jurisprudence, medicine, chemistry, geography, politics, and mantic, which is a Greek word that means "prophetic, inspired, or otherwise not coming from the human mind."

The Reverend Cramer went onto explain that the reason these manuscripts were so important is that they included much of the recorded history of the Ottoman Empire. These manuscripts covered a wide range of topics, including the following:

- History: Official histories of the Ottoman Empire, written by some of the empire's most important historians.
- Legal texts: Such as deeds of ownership and decrees.
- Astronomy, biology, physics, faith, mathematics, and mysticism.
- Greek medical treatises: These treatises included folk remedies, astrological medicine, and lists of good-luck and bad-luck days for bloodletting. (Bloodletting, also known as phlebotomy or venesection, was a therapeutic procedure that involves removing blood from a person to treat a medical condition. It has been practiced for at least three thousand years and was a common treatment until the nineteenth century.)

Reverend Michael stressed what he had learned of this art/manuscript theft ring. Because the Ottoman Empire was one of the mightiest and longest-lasting dynasties in world history, any type of manuscript was considered valuable, especially by any Islamic state in the Middle East, such as Turkey, Iran, Iraq, Jordan, and Egypt. (The Ottoman Islamic-run superpower ruled large areas of the Middle East, Eastern Europe, and North Africa for more than six hundred years.)

The manuscript that it was questioned was referred to as apart from *The History of Sultan Suleyman*. Also known as *The Book of Victory* or *Zafarname*, this manuscript was written by court historian Seyyid Lokman and illustrated by palace workshop artists. What is missing is not the whole manuscript but a few pages that include art illustrations that tell the story of the sultan. "This manuscript and the Emerald Dagger are missing, and this is why I believe," said Reverend Cramer, "the employees of Kevin are also missing."

As I listened to the reverend, I couldn't help but think about the note that was placed under my door warning me that those who chased the dagger would be brought down. I went to my desk in the room and pulled out the envelope and the note and shared them with the reverend.

Reverend Cramer looked surprised and, at the same time, puzzled. He said that these were the same types of tactics that were used upon him many

CHAPTER 8

years ago when he was trying to take down the art theft ring. "Interesting," I thought. I still wasn't entirely convinced that the reverend was on my side. He had never really answered why he was back here in Istanbul and what was he looking for. I was beginning to ask myself the question, "Just whom can I trust?"

I thanked the reverend for all his history lesson and told him about Nancy being killed late last night and about her message that the manuscript the artifact and the employees could all be found at the Blue Mosque. The reverend didn't seem to upset or surprised at what I told him. I asked him if he would like to go with the group of travelers that we were assembling in the lobby of this hotel at 9:00 a.m., which was less than an hour away. The reverend said he would love to come.

The reverend quickly said his goodbye and left me standing in my room, wondering about the exchange that had taken place and still trying to understand why the reverend was here in Istanbul. Yes, I know he was on a sabbatical from his Unitarian congregation in Los Angeles, but why come to Istanbul unless he had a score to settle? Here was the start of my second day in Istanbul, and I still had no clue as to what was going on two murders to solve and a slew of unanswered questions.

I glanced across the room at my bedside clock. It read 8:45. I had better get a move on it if I was going to make it down to the lobby by 9:00 a.m. I forwent a shower or shaving and quickly dressed and took one look in the mirror to make sure that I looked OK. My hair was slicked back. I wore a bright maroon-colored club-type shirt with my blue jeans and my black lace-up boots. I was trying to look as if I had some type of dressing style and important. After all, I am the great "Inspector Sterling." I took one last look in the mirror and smiled. I was OK. I walked to the door, opened it, and walked out into the hall.

As I walked toward the elevator, I begin to review in my mind all the cast of characters I had encountered over the last few days. There was Mr. Jerry Davison, the general manager of the hotel. He and I had been very involved in the last case that I had worked on, and he was also a longtime old friend. He had been in Istanbul for less than a year, and I still hadn't got a reasonable explanation as to why he chooses Istanbul and this hotel to invest his time and expertise in. He had known about my meeting on the roof deck, and I

39

found that to be a bit puzzling since I had not spoken to him since he greeted me when I arrived.

Then there was Ms. Elizabeth Jackson. She had tried to purchase the Grand Hotel, where, in a previous case, she was very much involved even though she didn't commit any murder. She was a wealthy multimillionaire and claimed that she was here because she invested in the hotel as well as in Kevin's start-up business. I didn't trust her the last time that our paths crossed, and I certainly didn't trust her any more this time. She was someone that I would need to watch closely.

The Reverend Dr. Sterling Halt was there. He claimed because he had been hired by the Turkish government to offer his expertise regarding some of the Aramaic writing and has experience in dealing with real and forgery manuscripts. I didn't trust him the last time we interacted, and I still don't trust him. I just needed to learn why is he here in Istanbul, and he was another one to watch. My experience with him was that he got involved only when he saw that it was to his advantage, and he could make money.

What about my good friend Mustafa? Now he was someone I can trust, and he worked for the US embassy as a translator, but his family roots were a part of the Islamic culture. He also was a former bartender, so he knew how to gain people's trust. He was easy to talk with and very knowledgeable. He had gotten to know many of these characters better than I because he had been interacting with them longer than I had. He was also a no-nonsense kind of guy. He told you what he thought and didn't sugarcoat anything. I needed to spend some time with him.

Then there was my good friend Kevin. I was not sure what was going on with him, and I did believe that he was not telling me all that he knew. He had always been a very strategic planning type of person, and lately his behavior seemed to be off. I didn't see him being as strategic as I had known him to be in the past. I still felt and believed that something or someone was keeping him from sharing with me the whole story as to why he was here in Istanbul and what he had gotten himself involved with.

The elevator opened, and I made my way inside, pushed the button marked M, and off we went on a quick ride downward. The elevator quickly came to a stop. The doors opened, and I made my way into the lobby. I glanced at my watch, and it was right at 9:00 am. I saw Ms. Jackson siting down in the

CHAPTER 8

seating area in the middle of the lobby. I made my way to her, and she stood up and said, "Well, good morning, Inspector. How are you doing?"

I replied, "Well," and thanked her for asking and inquired as to if she would be joining the group I was assembling to travel to the Blue Mosque. She replied that something had come up at the last minute, but she had hoped that she could join us later that evening for dinner at the hotel at 7:00 p.m. Just then her cell phone rang, and she excused herself and walked away from me.

I sat down in one of the overstuffed chairs and looked up, and there was Reverend Cramer, walking and conversing with my friend Kevin, and they were walking toward me. I saw from the corner of my left eye Mr. Jerry Davison making his way across the lobby to where I was sitting. At just about the same time, all three-gentleman arrived, and I greeted them with a strong good morning greeting. Kevin looked surprised, and the other two made small grunt sounds.

I explained that I had spoken with Ms. Jackson and that she had something come up and so would not be joining us on our travel to the Blue Mosque but would like each of us to join her this evening at 7:00 p.m. for dinner at the hotel restaurant. Just then Mr. Davison received a call on his cell phone. He took the call and then said, "Hold on." He turned to all of us and said, "I am not going to join you something has come up here at the hotel. I will try and join you for dinner this evening." The three of us said our goodbyes, and Kevin and Reverend Cramer asked if Dr. Reverend Sterling Halt would be joining us. Just then Mr. Davison came back to inform the three of us that Dr. Halt had called and that he would meet us at the Blue Mosque. "How strange," I thought but let that thought slip quickly by my thought process.

From purely a historical point of view, I was excited to have the opportunity to see the Blue Mosque. The Blue Mosque was considered one of the last great mosques of the classic period of the Ottoman Empire. It was built with six minarets. A minaret is a type of tower typically built into or adjacent to mosques. Minarets are generally used to project the Muslim call to prayer from a muezzin, but they also served as landmarks and symbols of Islam's presence.

The mosque is called the Blue Mosque because its interior is lined with more than twenty thousand handmade titles. The mosque's upper levels are also painted blue, with natural light flooding in from the more than two hundred stained-glass windows. The Blue Mosque was a historical mosque in Istanbul. The mosque played a critical role in the Ottoman Empire. How odd that the mosque would be the place where we were directed to.

Kevin, Dr. Cramer, and I made our way outside of the hotel. According to our map, the mosque was only a five-to-six-minute walk from the hotel. In fact, as I looked to the right when came out of the hotel, I could see the towers of the mosque and the building itself. The three of us made our way. Kevin started talking as to where he thought we might first look when we got to the mosque. According to Kevin the courtyard would be a great place to start. The courtyard was right outside the mosque and surrounded the building. "We could take in a view of the mosque, taking time to appreciate the domes and the minarets. Moving into the mosque toward the prayer hall and the grand dome. The grand dome rises above the prayer hall, and it is supported by four large columns that are adorned with intricate geometric patterns and calligraphy."

It was becoming clearer to me that trying to find the kidnapped employees and the stolen artifact was not going to be easy, given the size of the Blue Mosque. None of us knew where to look or even how to move about in the mosque. I was surprised just how much Kevin knew, but he had said in an earlier conversation that he had been to the Blue Mosque on two other occasions.

As we rounded the next corner there, there was the Blue Mosque in all its grandeur. The mosque was magnificent looking in all its opulence. Kevin picked up his pace, and each of us followed. Within a minute or two, we found ourselves standing in the courtyard of the Blue Mosque. The three of us were preparing to go inside when we saw a young Muslim man dressed in a long white robe running toward us. He said that his name was Isbad and that he was a friend of Mustafa and that he would take us to where Mustafa was inside of the Blue Mosque. We followed the young man, as it seemed that we were all walking fast, almost a slow run. Once inside the Blue Mosque, I had to stop. As I looked around, I was surrounded by blue mosque tiles called "Iznik Tiles" The tiles, adorned the walls, pillars, and domes. These

CHAPTER 8

hand-painted tiles featured intricate floral patterns, geometric designs, and calligraphy. It was a stunning sight to behold. I found it to be a moment of taking my breath away.

I looked up and saw the dome, and then over in the far corner, I spotted Mustafa. He looked right at home, and he was wearing the traditional long white robe with a head covering. He greeted us all and welcomed us to the mosque. It was now about an hour before prayer time, so Mustafa said that we were free to walk about. While we were standing there, another young man came up to us and asked to speak to Inspector Sterling, I told him that I was Inspector Sterling. He paused and said that after the prayer time this afternoon, I was to wait in the prayer hall, and many of the questions I have would be answered. He indicated that since we were all non-Muslims, we would have to leave the mosque and could wait in the courtyard until prayer time had concluded. I asked him to tell me more, but that was all he said. Kevin and Dr. Cooper were somewhat startled, but after the young man waked away, they indicated that they would wait with me out of sight. I thought, "Another mystery and someone is in control of this. Who or where I do not know, but I will find out." We all agreed to make our way to the prayer hall and to the outside courtyard to wait for the end of prayer time.

The spacious prayer hall inside the mosque had several large and semi-domes, creating a sense of depth and grandeur within the monument. As we walked among the domes, we couldn't help but appreciate the harmonious blend of light, space, and design among the domes. The prayer hall itself was punctuated with several architectural features, including the sultan's platform and an arcaded gallery running along the interior walls except on the qibla wall facing Mecca. A carved marble niche set into the center of this wall guided the faithful to the correct direction for prayer. To its right was a tall and thin marble pulpit (minbar) capped with an ornamental turret.

The courtyard's inner frame was a domed arcade, which was uniform on all sides except for the prayer hall entrance, where the arches expanded. Inside, the central dome rested on delicate pendentives (triangular segments of a spherical surface) with its weight supported on four massive, fluted columns. To extend the prayer space beyond the span of the central dome, a series of half domes cascaded outward from the center to ultimately join the exterior walls of the mosque. Of the six minarets (towers traditionally built for the call to prayer), four were positioned on the corners of the mosque's prayer hall, while the other two flanked the external corners of the courtyard. Each of these "pencil" minarets had a series of balconies adorning its lean form.

Once inside the inner courtyard, the three of us quietly stood against the far wall and waited for the prayer time to be finished. I had learned from Mustafa that prayer time ended by having every present recite the Taslim. The Taslim (تسليم) was the concluding portion of the salah, where one recites السلام عليكم ورحمة الله "As-salāmu alaikum wa-raḥmatu-llah" ("Peace and blessings of God be unto you") and in Sunni Islam, once while facing the right, and once while facing the left.

Mustafa had previously informed me that on average the prayer time lasted about thirty minutes, and the Jumu'ah prayer lasted around ten minutes. After the prayers it was common for members of the congregation to gather and greet each other as they were leaving the mosque. I looked at my watch. It was now 1:00 p.m., and if all went well, prayer time should end in about thirty minutes.

I thought, "So much mystery still to be solved and so many questions to be answered. Three murders, two missing employees and a missing Ottoman artifact, not to mention the previous national case of missing art from the National Turkey Gallery." Somewhere between all of this, there had to be a connection. The killing of Selim at the Munich airport, then the throat slashing of one of Kevin's kidnapped employees, and finally the brutal murder of Nancy, who, from what I could tell, was only acting as a messenger. I kept going over the events and the people that I had been in contact with over the past twenty-four to thirty-six hours. I failed to see the connection between the deaths.

I had been asked by Kevin to come here and help him find his kidnapped employees as a well as the missing Ottoman artifact. I stood quietly with Dr. Cramer beside me, Kevin a few feet away and Mustafa inside the prayer hall, participating in noontime prayer. I glanced at my watch again. It was almost 1:30. Prayer time should be ending. I heard what I thought was the chime of a bell, although I doubted it had come from inside the mosque. It sounded more like it was coming from the Christian church across the street.

I looked across the courtyard and saw my friend Mustafa motioning for us to come to him. I turned to Kevin and Dr. Cramer and said, "Let's go."

CHAPTER 8

We slowly quickened our pace and made it across the vast courtyard into the prayer hall, where Mustafa was standing. Mustafa said for us to follow him. We made our way back into the great prayer hall, and in the far corner directly across the room were two people who looked very calm yet purposeful. They were waiting for the three of us.

They introduced themselves as Dr. Umar Abadi and Dr. Salma Amin. In Arabic, last names of people are based on their tribe, clan, place, and origin of their family. I was surprised to learn that Dr. Salam was a woman and that her last name meant "truthful." They both, for a moment, stood in silence, then Dr. Salma spoke. "We bring you a message from the kidnappers. The two employees are well, and the Emerald Dagger is safe. They are willing to exchange the artifact and the two employees but are requiring that a blood sacrifice be made as a sign of obedience to honor the Muslim holiday of Eid al-Adha, which is celebrated to commemorate Prophet Abraham's willingness to sacrifice his son as an act of obedience to Allah. It symbolizes faith, devotion, and submission to Allah's commands. The celebration serves as a reminder of the importance of sacrifice, gratitude, and caring for others in the Muslim faith."

Dr. Umar chimed in to say that we had a choice. We could offer one of us as the sacrifice, or they would choose one of the kidnapped employees or would choose to kill one of us on their own as a sign of sacrifice. Dr. Salam spoke again and said that the kidnappers were giving us forty-eight hours to decide, and if we chose to offer the sacrifice, we were to go to the Bosporus, also known as the Strait of Istanbul, which is a natural strait that runs through the city of Istanbul. The Bosporus is about nineteen miles long and twenty-three hundred feet wide, and it connects the Black Sea to the Sea of Marmara. The Bosporus is a strategic waterway that has been important to world maritime trade for centuries.

We were to bring our sacrifice to the Maiden's Tower (Turkish: Kız Kulesi), also known as Leander's Tower (Tower of Leandros) since the medieval Byzantine perio. It is a tower lying on a small islet located at the southern entrance of the Bosporus strait 200 meters (220 yards) from the coast of Üsküdar in Istanbul, Turkey. We were to arrive their and wait for further instructions. I tried to push the two doctors into giving us more information as to where and how they became the messengers, and all that they said was they had been contacted by a party who was staying at our hotel and were asked if they could deliver the message. They assured us that they had no connection to the kidnappers or to the other individuals that had been a part of our team.

The two messengers turned and started walking quickly out of the mosque. I turned to Kevin and Dr. Cramer and said, "Now what?" All of us were feeling overwhelmed and needed to just process all that had occurred. Kevin stated, "Why don't we try and find Mustafa and head back to the hotel and regroup at the bar? Somehow a good drink can help to clear the air and gain greater clarity." Together we walked slowly out of the mosque. I saw Mustafa walking ahead of us and called out his name, He turned around and looked puzzled until our eyes connected.

I said, "Wait up." The four of us walked slowly back to the hotel in silence, trying to process all that had occurred and the message that we had been given. Someone was in control of all these happenings, and if I could only figure that out, I did believe that the rest would all begin to make sense. As a seasoned inspector, I rarely got stumped, but I must admit this whole case had me stumped. The answer was somewhere I just needed time to figure it all out and to think about who is in charge. Who was making me and the rest jump through hoops?

Just then we arrived at the hotel, and I spied Mr. Davison, the manager, and motioned for him. He made his way over, and I asked if we could meet later that evening around 8:30 p.m. He said we could meet in his office. I turned to Kevin and Dr. Cramer and Mustafa and said, "I will join you in the bar in about ten minutes. I want to look at the roof top restaurant bar again."

CHAPTER 9

THE BOSPORUS STRAIT

I left Mustafa, Dr. Cramer, and Kevin and made my way to the rooftop elevator. I needed to check out the roof deck bar and once again look at the scene where Nancy had been meeting with me and then ended up being murdered. I waited for the elevator to arrive. Out of the corner of my eye, I witnessed Ms. Jackson having what appeared to be a heated exchange with Mr. Jerry Davison, the hotel manager. It looked as if Ms. Jackson was not happy. Just then the elevator opened, and I pushed the button for the roof deck, and off I went.

"How odd," I thought, "that Ms. Jackson, would be so upset with Mr. Davison." My previous experience in dealing with her was that she was very demanding, but usually if you could at least meet her halfway in what she was demanding, she could deal with that. Of course, I never really trusted her when I came across her in my last case and still find it hard to believe her story that she is just an investor in our hotel. She had a way of getting involved in business deals that were not always aboveboard, and she had an uncanny ability to fold out of the deal if she believed that it is not going to benefit her.

The elevator stopped, and the door opened to the roof deck restaurant and bar. I gazed out and tried to see if there was any other easy way that one could arrive at the roof deck other than the elevator. I noticed what appeared to be a manager who was making his way to me from across the deck. He said, "Inspector Sterling, welcome. What can I do for you?" I mentioned that I was there just to look around and to see if I could find any type of clue that would give me some idea of just how the murderer was able to get to Nancy.

I asked if there was any other way to get to the restaurant other than the elevator. Jared, that was his name, said, "Well, there is a stairway that goes to the floor below, which contains four corner suites." He said that one of the suites is the residence of Mr. Jerry Davison, the general manager of the hotel, and another is being used by Ms. Jackson who is one of the main investors of the hotel. I asked Jared if he could take me down the stairs to the next level. Jared called out to one of his employees and asked if he could be on watch and that he would be right back. Jared turned to me and said, "Follow me." He opened a door that was right behind the elevator, and there was a series of stairs that descended to another level. At the bottom of the stairs was a blue door. Jared opened the door and waved for me to follow him. Once on the other side of the door was a hallway. Jared pointed to the left and said, "See that door at the end of the hallway?"

"Yes," I replied.

"That is the door that goes into the suite of Ms. Jackson," Jared said. "On the other side of the hallway is the door that goes into the suite of Mr. Davison, our general manager."

I looked up at the ceiling and noticed in the far corners a camera. I asked Jared if he had access to the cameras and if they had a tape. He said that there is a control room behind the front desk at the hotel, and it has various views coming from the many cameras around the hotel. He said that he would check with the front desk and tell them that I would come down and look over the tapes. I thanked him and made my way back to the stairs and quickly climbed them back to the roof deck. I had found a clue; I was excited to look over the tapes to see if they would show me anything. Whoever killed Nancy the stairs would provide them an easy exit. I walked back the stairs and turned in front of the Elevator.

Just then the bell rang, and the elevator opened its door. I got inside and pushed the button to the main floor. The elevator descended quickly, and within no time at all, I was once again waiting for the elevator doors to open for the main floor. I heard the bell, and the elevator stopped, the doors opened, and I stepped out only to run right into Mr. Davison. I practically

CHAPTER 9

knocked him over, but he quickly recovered and asked me, "What can I do for you, Inspector?"

I replied, "I need to look at your camera tapes, especially the ones from the hallways on the floor right down from the roof top restaurant."

Mr. Davison, looked right at me and said, "Why do you need to look at those tapes? I doubt very much if you will find anything of value on them."

I responded, "Let me be the judge of that."

Mr. Davison finally said, "I certainly won't stand in your way of your murder investigation."

Jerry motioned for me to follow him, and I started following him. As we got closer to the front check in desk, I looked over into my left into the hotel bar. Kevin, Mustafa, Rev. Cramer, and Dr. Halt were all gathered at the bar. I got Mustafa's eye and waved for him to come to me. Mustafa quickly got up and made his way to me. Mr. Davidson had made it to the front desk and turned around to see if I was right behind him. I let Mustafa know that I would be joining all in his party in about a half hour.

Mr. Jerry Davison led me through the door and into the security room where all the camera images were being displayed. He went to one of the terminals by the far screen and typed in the hours from 9:30 p.m. to 11:30 p.m. the night before, and the screen went dark, and then quickly I saw the images of the floor that I had been on a few hours ago. I saw Mr. Davison go into this his suite and then nothing until 11:05 p.m. The door opened and it was Ms. Jackson. She walked toward the door that had the stairs that went to the roof deck restaurant. I saw her open the door and the door close. I waited and watched. About ten minutes later, I saw the door open, and Ms. Jackson stepped into the hall, ran quickly to her door suite, and opened it, and then nothing again until midnight. And Mr. Davison came out of his door and hurried toward the stair door. That time was around the same time that I called Kevin, after I had discovered Nancy's body. I wondered where Ms. Jackson was going when she took the stairs. I was looking forward to confronting Ms. Jackson about this.

I left the security room and walked out and over to the hotel bar. Mustafa, Dr. Halt, Rev. Cramer, and Kevin were all deeply engrossed in conversation when I approached them. Mustafa was busily explaining to Dr. Halt all the events that had occurred while all of us were at the Blue Mosque. Kevin was loudly conversing with Rev. Cramer about the Emerald Dagger and why it was such a valuable artifact from the Ottoman Empire. I wasn't sure how I was going to enter any of the conversations, but when they all finally saw me, they stopped talking and asked, "What did you learn that you didn't already know?"

I began to explain how I learned about the stairs from the roof deck that led to a lower level and how on the security footage I saw Ms. Jackson take the stairs up to the roof deck and take them back all in less than ten minutes. Kevin spoke up immediately and said, "I for one don't trust Ms. Elizabeth Jackson." Mustafa said that he remembered her from a previous work assignment, and she was very strategic in all that she did or went after.

If Ms. Jackson killed Nancy, why? And how was that murder connected to the other one at the Munich airport as well as Kevin's employee? Nancy was a strong and smart businesswoman, and I needed to understand why she might get involved with people like Ms. Jackson, and what was Nancy's connection to Istanbul. There had to be a strong reason for Ms. Jackson to be here and to have possibility killed Nancy. I would have to confront Ms. Jackson. Lately it seemed that wherever Mr. Davison was, Ms. Elizabeth Jackson was not far behind.

I turned to the group of Kevin, Mustafa, Dr. Cramer, Dr. Halt and said, "I need to find Ms. Jackson. Have any of you have seen her recently?" Mustafa spoke up and related that he had seen her having a coffee at the bakery next to the hotel. I excused myself from the group and made my way to the hotel lobby and out the door. As I recalled, the Turkish bakery was right next to the right of the hotel. I exited the hotel and turned to my right and started walking. I quickly picked up my pace to make sure that I would be able to catch Ms. Jackson.

In no time at all, I was in front of the bakery, and as I looked in, I spied Ms. Jackson talking with an unknown gentleman, and they appeared to be having a heated discussion. I made my way to the front door of the bakery and pushed the door inward and looked over to the right. Ms. Jackson caught my eye and quickly motioned for me to come over. She looked somewhat relieved to have a familiar face coming toward her. The man who appeared to be Middle Eastern with his dark black hair and beard quickly got up from the

CHAPTER 9

table, and I heard him say, "You have been warned," and then he quickly ran for the door and was gone.

I stood there feeling somewhat perplexed as to what I just witnessed. Ms. Jackson motioned for me to sit down and join her. As I sat down, I looked directly at Ms. Jackson, and I saw fear in her eyes. My reasoning for finding her to confront her regarding Nancy's murder quickly went to that of trying to calm her regarding the exchange that happened in front of me. We both sat there in silence for the next few minutes. Ms. Jackson than said, "I guess I owe you an explanation?"

I paused, and she went on to say, "I have gotten involved in a situation that is well over my head, and I am not sure how to untangle the mess that I find myself in."

I nodded my head as if to say, "OK, go on." She than begin to talk about when she heard about the opportunity to invest in Kevin's company, she was intrigued. She had always been a fan of the arts and history especially Ottoman history. When she learned that Kevin's company traded in Ottoman artifacts as well as connected art dealers who were interested in buying and selling Turkish art and especially Ottoman artifacts, she wanted in. She met Ahmet Yilmaz, Kevin's vice president of Hao Technologies. She was interested.

I asked how she has met Mr. Yilmaz, and she said that Kevin had introduced them on one of her many trips to Istanbul. She hired an investigator to check into his background as well as Kevin's. She learned that Mr. Yilmaz had been questioned about the missing manuscripts and famous Turkish art, but authorities were never able to find any real evidence that connected him to the crime of stealing the three hundred pieces of art and making copies of many and then replacing them back in the museums as the real pieces. Only three individuals had been charged and went to prison, and fifteen others were never charged.

"What excited me most," said Ms. Jackson, "was the Emerald Dagger." Kevin through his connections had found a dealer who was willing to put the Ottoman artifact up for sale. I had learned a little bit about the dagger from Dr. Reverend Sterling Halt, the noted theologian with an expertise in Aramaic inscriptions. He told me that the dagger is known for its exquisite craftsmanship and historical significance.

These daggers were often ornately decorated with intricate designs, including floral motifs, calligraphy, and geometric patterns. They were crafted by skilled artisans and often adorned with precious materials such as gold, silver, and gemstones. The Emerald Dagger typically served as a symbol of status and prestige. Beyond their aesthetic beauty, they also held cultural and historical significance, representing the martial prowess and opulence of the Ottoman Empire.

Ms. Jackson continued with her story. Kevin introduced me to Selim Aksu, who was believed by Turkish authorities to be the mastermind behind the original art thefts. Selim was the gentleman who greeted me outside my condo in Chicago and whom Nancy and I saw get murdered at the airport in Munich. Ms. Jackson went on further to explain that Kevin had introduced her to Emiri Tarkin, who was the art curator at the Topkapi Place, where in the basement Kevin, Emiri, Selim and Ahmet all agreed they would hold an art show and display the Emerald Dagger.

Ms. Jackson agreed to be one of the sponsors of the show and was looking forward to the show opening. The night before the opening at the Topkapi Place Emiri was found with his throat slit in the basement of the palace, and Amet was found a few days later in the main train station in downtown Istanbul with his throat slit. "I suggested to Kevin that he reach out to you, Inspector, and ask for your assistance in trying to solve these murders and to also recover the two staff members of Kevin's company that were missing."

Ms. Jackson further went onto state that she had gotten connected with Ms. Nancy Donaldson, and had persuaded her to take the new contract job at the hotel and at Kevin's company. She explained to Nancy that both organizations need a strong financial individual who could wade through the financial records and find ways in which both the hotel and Kevin's start-up company could make money. Ms. Jackson continued to explain that Nancy had reached out to her to inform her that the financial records at the hotel were showing that embezzlement had been occurring over the past several years and that the value on the books had been greatly inflated when her and Mr. Jerry Davison started looking at purchasing the hotel.

Nancy further explained that it appeared that money from the sale of art was being passed through the revenue and expenses of the hotel but had stopped when she and Mr. Davison had taken over the management of the hotel. "Nancy was hired by me to do an in-depth look at the financial records and to create a money trail as to where the money came from and where it went over the past ten years. Before Nancy had arrived in Istanbul, she had discovered the money trail and who was behind it. She had arranged to meet me in my hotel room after midnight. When she hadn't arrived, I went up to the roof deck to connect with her or to see if she was already there. I had learned that earlier in the evening she had received a crypted message, and it said that she was to deliver to you the news where the employees of Kevin's company were being held and where the Emerald Dagger could be found.

"I learned later from Mr. Jerry Davison that she was meeting you on the roof deck at midnight. I went up to the roof deck using the staircase located in my hallway of where my room was at. I walked up to the roof deck looked around and walked back. I figured that you would be tracking me down because Mr. Davison told me that you had looked over the security tapes. I did not kill Nancy, and I have no idea who did because Nancy was never able to go over what she had discovered with me."

I sat there having listened to Ms. Jackson, and she had provided me with some of the connections, but I still found myself with a lot of unanswered questions. It was clear to me that Ms. Jackson would not have killed Nancy because she needed Nancy to share with her what she had discovered in the financial records. I asked Ms. Jackson about the conversation that I had witnessed and about the man who had said to her. "You have been warned." Ms. Jackson took a deep breath and then said that she had received a note stating that the employees and the Emerald Dagger were being held in the Maiden's Tower or Leander's Tower, which is in the middle of the Bosporus Strait. Ms. Jackson also said that the kidnappers are requiring a blood sacrifice, and this is to honor the Muslim holiday of Eid al-Adha, which is a holiday to celebrate the sacrifice that the Prophet Abraham made as an act of obedience to Allah.

The unknown gentleman had sought out Ms. Jackson at the bakery and told her that he was a messenger from the kidnappers and that if she didn't provide a blood sacrifice that the kidnappers would take matters into their own hands. He ended his monologue by saying to me, "You have been warned." I shared with Ms. Jackson that I had received the same message from when I and my party were in the Blue Mosque. I invited Ms. Jackson to follow me back to the hotel, and there we would hold a meeting with Kevin,

Mustapha, Dr. Crammer, and Dr. Halt to strategize just how we were going to approach these next forty-eight hours.

Ms. Jackson and I got up from our table at the bakery and made our way to the door, went through, and started our walk back to the hotel. I asked her, once we arrived, if she could arrange for Mr. Davison to meet with us as well at the bar in the hotel restaurant.

CHAPTER 10

MAIDEN'S TOWER

Ms. Jackson's and our short walk back to the hotel was a quiet one. I asked her how she was feeling, and she responded, "I'm scared to death." I assured her that I would do all in my power to make sure that nothing would happen to her. She thanked me and continued to look straight ahead. All I could hear was the sound of her quick breaths as we continued to walk side by side back to the hotel. Once we got to the main entrance, Ms. Jackson turned to me and said, "Do you remember the Reverend Janice Turner? I met her at the conference in the Catskills of New York and you got to know her when working on your last case?" I remembered the Reverend Janice, and if I recall correctly, she came from an international marketing company that was Swiss owned before she came into the ministry. Ms. Jackson responded yes. I asked why she was bringing her up. Ms. Jackson went on further to state that she had run into Rev. Turner and Revered Austin (whose partner had been killed a little over a year ago). They were now both working in Istanbul doing ministry, and on the side, they had started a business buying and trading in Ottoman artifacts and Turkish artwork.

I looked puzzled, and the hotel door opened, and Ms. Jackson walked through, and I followed close behind. I asked Ms. Jackson if she knew where I could find the two reverend's she replied, "I believe that they are staying at the Sultanhan Hotel." I believed that it just minutes from the Grand Bazaar,

Hagia Sophia, the Blue Mosque and Topkapi Palace, I thought. Hum, I wonder what the two of them are doing in Istanbul and am curious about this new business venture that they have started. Ms. Jackson excused herself and said that she was going to go find Mr. Jerry Davison and ask him to meet us in the hotel bar.

I slowly made my way across the lobby over to the hotel bar, which was in the far corner, from a distance I could see my friend Kevin, Both Dr. Cramer and Dr. Holt. Kevin caught my eye and motioned for me to come and join them. I sat down with them, and everyone spoke at once and wanted to know how my meeting went with Ms. Jackson. I quickly shared that we still didn't know who killed Nancy, but it wasn't Ms. Jackson. I went onto say that many of my unanswered questions had been cleared up by Ms. Jackson, as she explained a lot of things, but I still have more questions and now knowing that two more people from my last case are in town I have more questions. I told them I was hoping that Mr. Davison could shed some light onto some of my questions.

I ordered a round of drinks for everyone, and I looked up and saw Ms. Jackson and Mr. Davison coming across the lobby to all of us in a very rushed state with upset expressions on their faces.

Mr. Davison got to us and was quickly followed by Ms. Jackson; Mr. Davison was holding onto a crude note that had been made with cut out letters from what appeared to be a type of catalog.

"The art of the Ottomans before 1600." Had been stamped on the back of the crudely organized note. The note simply said, we are waiting to exchange the Emerald Dagger and the hostages but are requiring a blood sacrifice, please plan to meet us before Sundown today at the Maiden Tower. (The **Maiden's Tower** also known as **Leander's Tower** is a tower on a small islet at the southern entrance of the Bosporus strait).

Kevin had a look on his face of terror. He wanted his employees back safe, and he also wanted to recover the dagger but didn't want anyone to die in the process. There was a series of words that were written in Arabic and Dr. Sterling Holt tried to translate them but had a hard time. I asked where Mustafa was, he would be able to translate the words. He had followed our group back from the Blue Mosque, but I had not seen him this morning. Dr.

CHAPTER 10

Michael Cramer offered to text him which he did and asked him to join us in the hotel bar. In a manner of minutes Mustafa showed up and he looked at the Arabic words and was able to decipher them. "He said, "It is two words that mean the same thing but are used in different ways. The words were ud-hiya and qurban. Mustafa went onto explain that the Arabic word for "blood sacrifice" is udhiya. In Islamic law, udhiya is also known as qurbān, which is an Arabic word that means "an act performed to seek Allah's pleasure." Qurbani is an Urdu and Persian word that comes from the Arabic word qurban and is used to describe the sacrifice of an animal for Allah.

Mustafa went onto explain that whoever sent this note is expecting some type of blood sacrifice which could ether be a human or an animal. This left us all somewhat perplexed and in a quandary. We were not going to sacrifice a human, and we were in no place to sacrifice an animal. We had the next few hours to figure out what we were going to do. Kevin spoke up first and pleaded that getting his employees back alive was the most important and the dagger would be an added extra.

Mustafa said that he would come with us and prepare a blood sacrifice of a goat. "I am familiar with Maiden's tower and know how to get in and out of the meeting place quickly. Ms. Jackson, Dr. Holt and Dr. Cramer were anxious to come along as well. Mr. Jerry Davison said that he would alert the authorities as to what we are dealing with and would stay behind at the hotel but would stay in contact by way of texting. The five of us agreed to meet at 5:00 p.m. in the hotel lobby to begin our travel to the Maiden Tower.

"Mustafa reminded us all that the tower is situated on a small islet, so it can be accessed by boat only. There are two departure points. One from the European side and the other one from the Asian side of Istanbul." We all agreed that we would meet on the European side and take the ferry out to the tower.

I looked up and over at our group. I hoped that no one in this group was guilty of committing a murder but at this point I had to be careful of everyone and not give anyone the benefit of the doubt. Kevin felt strongly that we do not contact the Istanbul police, where I on the other hand believed that it was a good caution to at least make them aware of what was happening Mustafa and Dr. Cramer also agreed with me. Reverend Dr. Michael Cramer had a contact at the police that he had worked with years ago when he was in the FBI. He said that he would see if some under cover back up could be provided for us.

We all said our goodbyes and agreed to meet back together in about four hours. I wanted to follow up and see if I could contact Reverend Janice and Reverend Austin who Ms. Jackson claimed were staying at the Sultan Hotel. I stopped at the front desk of the hotel to ask for directions to the Sultan Hotel. The manager at the front desk informed me that the Sultan Hotel was within a short walk from my hotel. It was about four hundred meters from the Blue Mosque or right down the street, less than a five-minute walk. I thanked the kind gentleman who helped me and turned and walked across the lobby and out the door onto the street. I was going to use this time to see if I could connect with the two reverends and learn why they were here and what they were up to.

I turned right when I left the hotel and started walking, I noticed the Blue Mosque, and in the distance on the opposite side of the street, I saw what I thought could be the hotel. Within a manner of a minute, I was standing on the oppositive of the street looking upon the Sultan Hotel. As I gazed upon the hotel, I noticed that the exterior reflected the traditional Ottoman architecture with ornate domes, arched windows, and intricate decorative motifs. The main entrance was adorned with intricate tile work along with stone embellishments including moldings, reliefs, and small pieces of contrasting stone. It was truly an artistical wonder to look upon.

I quickly ran across the street and there waiting at the entrance of the hotel was a traditional door man who politely said, "Welcome to our hotel." He opened the door, and I entered an impressive, large lobby around four hundred to five hundred meters high. The walls were decorated with Ottoman-style textiles and antiques and original historical wooden pieces could be seen spaced just right around the lobby area. All in all, it was a welcoming sight, and I felt a sense of belonging and peace that I had not experienced since arriving in Istanbul.

After I had taken the sight of the interior of the hotel in, I found my way to the front desk and inquired if I could have them ring ether Reverend Janice Turners room or the Reverend Austin Roper's room. They asked me who was calling, I replied, "Inspector Sterling." The front desk attendant called

CHAPTER 10

Ms. Reverend Turner's room first, and there was no answer. She then tried Reverend Roper's room, and there was no answer there as well. She asked me if I could leave a message with her as to where I could be contacted; she would relay the information. I told her that it was Inspector Sterling, and I am staying at the Hotel Miughaamara in Room 401 and to please give me a call.

I found a seat in the lobby and sat down and went over the facts in the case that I had been able to determine so far. Nancy had been killed because of the information that she had discovered in the hotel books as well as Kevin's books. That information had to be incriminating to someone for them to take the action to kill her. Nancy had somewhat laid out how Ahmet and Shilm were all connected, and their killings appeared to have to do with the art theft and transfer of Turkish masterpieces and forgeries back in 2008 through 2011, which corresponds to the time when Reverend Michael Cooper was living in Istanbul and working for the FBI.

Then we have the connection between Ms. Elizabeth Jackson and Mr. Jerry Davison, the manager and owners of the hotel. I still haven't gotten a clear answer as to why Dr. Reverend Sterling Halt would choose to take his sabbatical year and spend it in Istanbul, Turkey. Mustafa is here as well working as an interpreter for the US Embassy. And how if any does he relate into the mix of this murder mystery? The latest mix that I still need to explore as to why Reverend Janice Turner and Reverend Austin Roper are here. There must be a connection between the art theft several years ago, the theft and disappearance of the Emerald Dagger, and the kidnapping of Kevin's employees. My years of solving cases taught me that there is always a connection, yet it always isn't the most noticeable but comes to attention after some careful thought.

I closed my eyes to think and felt myself slowly drifting away.

CHAPTER 11

OLD FRIENDS

I awoke hearing people talking in a loud manner. For the next several seconds, I felt as if I were floating and wondered if I had been asleep or just daydreaming. I started to regain my thought process and was brought out of the fog by the sound of a phone ringing. I made my way across the room to the phone, picked it up, and said, "Hello?"

The voice on the other end stated, "Inspector Sterling?"

"Yes," I said.

"This is Reverend Janice Turner. I received your message when I came in just now. You asked for me to call?"

"Yes," I said. "It is my understanding that you and the Reverend Austin Roper are here in Istanbul, and I was wondering if the three of us could meet? I am in the hotel lobby now if you are free."

Janice paused and said, "Sure. I will see you in about ten minutes."

"Great," I said. "Looking forward to it."

While sitting there waiting, my mind began to race through a series of questions that I would have to ask the good reverend. It was interesting that Ms. Jackson made a point to tell me that both Janice and Austin were here in Istanbul. I recalled that Janice before she became a minister worked in international marketing, and I believe it was a Swiss company. Austin, I recalled, was part of the foreign legion and spent time in South Africa and perhaps also

CHAPTER 11

in the Middle East. It was odd that both along with Ms. Jackson just happen to be here at the same time. I learned a long time ago in my work that there are no coincidences. Ms. Jackson and the Reverends Turner and Roper are here together for a reason, and I will discover that reason. It may take me a while, but I will.

As I looked across the lobby, I saw two figures making their way across the lobby to me. As they got closer, I recognized Reverend Roper and Reverend Tanner. They appeared to be smiling and at the same time moving quickly toward where I was sitting. Reverend Roper spoke first. "Good afternoon, Inspector. What brings you to Istanbul?"

Before I could answer him, Reverend Janice spoke up. "He's here on a case. Isn't that right, Inspector?"

I nodded my head and then asked both, "Why are both of you here?"

There was a big pause, and both looked at each other wondering who would answer my question. Finally, Reverend Roper spoke and said, "We are here doing research on the Ottoman Empire, and since Istanbul was at the heart of it, we decided that we would come here and see what we can find."

"And what have you found?" I asked.

Janice responded first by quickly saying, "Well, we are discovering a link between Islam and Christianity."

Reverend Roper quickly piped in and said, "Well Judaism, Christianity, and Islam all recognize Abraham as their first prophet."

"Yes," I said. "We call these the Abrahamic religions."

I looked directly at Reverend Janice and Reverend Roper and said, "Why are you really here in Istanbul?" Silence fell between us, and it seemed like both were searching for an answer.

Reverend Roper responded first by saying, "Well, we are interested in the Ottoman history, and particularly the history about the Emerald Dagger. We planned our trip to Istanbul to see the famous artifact, only to learn upon our arrival that it had disappeared."

I asked them if they knew the history about the Emerald Dagger. Reverend Roper said, "No. What about it?"

I then went onto explain, "The dagger, more commonly known as the Emerald Dagger, usually resides in Istanbul's Topkapi Palace Museum. It was brought out of storage to be the center piece on display for the Ottoman art and artifacts display taking place in the Topkapi Place Museum. The dagger has a history, dating back to the eighteenth century during the reign of Sultan Mahmud I. The Emerald Dagger was crafted as a gift for the Persian ruler Nadir Shah. It was part of a diplomatic mission aimed at strengthening ties between the Ottoman Empire and Persia. The dagger is renowned for its luxurious design, featuring three large emeralds set into the handle, surrounded by diamonds, and an intricate sheath adorned with enamel and additional gemstones.

I went on further to explain, "In 1747, while in route to deliver this and other gifts to Nadir Shah, the Ottoman delegation learned of Nadir Shah's assassination. The mission was aborted to prevent the treasures from being looted, and the dagger was brought back to Istanbul, where it was placed in the Topkapi Palace treasury. Today, the Emerald Dagger remains one of the museum's most famous artifacts, and when taken out of storage and put on display, it attracts numerous visitors who come to admire its craftsmanship and historical significance."

"I am here because of my longtime colleague and friend Kevin Hanes. He contacted me a few days ago and asked me to not only find the Emerald Dagger but to find his kidnapped employees. Kevin's company was sponsoring the art exhibit at the Topkapi Museum. The night before the exhibit was to open, the curator of the show was killed, and the dagger and Kevin's employees were kidnapped. Two murders have occurred so far that are related to the missing dagger. If the two of you know anything about this, now is the time to come forth and let me know."

Both reverends looked at each other and looked at me. Austin spoke up and said, "No, Inspector. We know nothing about the dagger or the kidnapped employees."

I asked them if they find anything in their research to let me know. I handed them my card and told them they could find me at the Miughaamara Hotel, Room 401. I got up from my chair, thanked them again, and made my way quickly to the door and exited. Once out on the street, I turned and looked through the windows. I could see what appeared to be the two exchanging words. Austin's gestures indicated that he was upset, and he kept throwing up his arms and madly pointing his fingers at Reverend Janice.

CHAPTER 11

Somehow my gut told me that they were not telling the truth, but I still had to find out just why they were in Istanbul and who if anyone they were working for. I quickened my step back in the direction to my hotel. I crossed the street and made my way to the door to the hotel, entered, and looked for a quiet place to sit. The large clock on one wall of the hotel indicted that the time was three thirty. I had just a half hour before we all were meeting.

My mind traced back over the events of the past few days. First the appearance of Selim outside my condo in Chicago and his assistance that he was there under direction from my friend Kevin. Selim must have escaped from the authorities and made his way to the United States. I remembered Kevin telling me that as soon as Selim arrived in Istanbul, the authorities would be waiting to arrest him. For the murder of the curator of the art show at the Topkapi Palace Museum. How did the authorities know that Selim would be landing in Istanbul? Someone knew and it appears that they had set Selim up.

Then to have Selim killed at the Munich airport brings up a lot of questions as to why, and again who knew that he would be traveling to Munich? If Selim was involved years before with the art thefts and forgery, then it appears that someone wanted him to be silenced. But why and how? It is clear to me that there just might be a group of people who are behind this and that somehow all of this is related to the missing Emerald Dagger and to Kevin's kidnapped employees.

Nancy paid the price with her death. What secrets are hidden in those financial records? What had Nancy found? These questions and others kept going through my mind. It was close to 4:00 p.m., our agreed time for all of us to meet. Mustafa had agreed to come along as our interpreter, and he was most familiar with the Maiden's Tower and would be able to provide us with incites as to where the kidnapers might be holding the employees and the famous dagger. I still wasn't sure about a blood sacrifice; we didn't have that covered, and none of us were going to be sacrificed for this cause.

I looked up from where I was sitting in the hotel lobby and saw Mustafa and Dr. Cramer making their way toward me. Dr. Holt was right behind them, along with Kevin. They all reached where I was around the same time and Kevin asked if we had seen Ms. Jackson. Mustafa said that he had spoken briefly with her about an hour ago and she was going to change her clothes and would meet him and the rest of us at 4:00 p.m. I wasn't surprised that she was late. She was the type of person that enjoyed making a grand entrance, so I was sure that she would appear shortly in the next few minutes.

The five of us exchanged pleasantries and waited patiently for Ms. Jackson. By 4:20 p.m., I began to get concerned and made a call to Jerry the hotel owner to ask if he had seen Ms. Jackson. He responded that she had left a message with him that she would meet all of us at the entrance to the tower at 5:00 p.m. I quickly shared that information with the others, and we all started walking toward the hotel exits and onto the street. We had about a twenty-minute walk, and Kevin led the procession, followed by Mustafa and Dr. Holt, then Dr. Cramer and I brought up the rear.

Our street path took us by the famous Blue Mosque. It seemed like days since we had visited that place, yet it had only been a few hours. So much had occurred, and I still remember the message. In exchange for the kidnapped employees, there had to be a blood sacrifice. We were going to be showing up without that sacrifice, but Kevin seemed to think that the kidnappers were not serious and that we would still be able to obtain the release of his employees.

Our pace accelerated, and we were getting closer to the area known as the Bosporus Strait. As we began to approach the tower, we could see the Galata Tower. The Galata Tower was built in the twelfth century and has served as an observatory, a jail, and a watchtower. It sits in the Bosporus Strait and has a great view of the Maiden's Tower in the small island that that tower sits on. Mustafa said it would be a great place for us to assemble and wait for the kidnappers before we take the boat ride out to the Maiden's Tower.

We arrived at the base of the Galata Tower. Mustafa suggested that Dr. Cramer and he go up in the tower and see what they can see from above in looking at the Bosporus Strait and especially the boat lunch where we would have to board a boat out to the Maiden's Tower. Mustafa and Dr. Cramer made their way inside the Galata Tower, and Kevin, Dr. Holt, and I stayed behind. We would need to board a boat to ride out to the island where the Maiden's Tower was. Once we were on the island, the only way off was to catch a ride back on another boat. I looked at Kevin. The expression on his face said that he was extremely worried and that he wondered how this exchange was going to turn out. After all it was his employees that were missing, and it was his show that he had sponsored to showcase Ottoman and other

CHAPTER 11

artifacts with the Emerald Dagger being the star of the show. Kevin looked at me and said, "Inspector, I am sorry that I ever got you involved in this mess. I never had any idea that it would turn into these murders and these strange meetings with these unknown individuals." I assured him that together we would solve this and that the employees along with the famous Ottoman artifact would be recovered.

Mustafa and Dr. Cramer had reached the top of the tower, and Mustafa texted me to say, "We can see some type of movement happening at the base of the Maiden's Tower." I told Kevin and said it was time for all of us to find the boat, board it, and ride out to the island where the tower sits on. Kevin and I left for the island, and Dr. Holt stayed behind and said he would go up and join Mustafa and Dr. Cramer. Kevin and I exchanged our greetings, and I texted Mustafa to let him know that we were on our way and to keep a watch on what was happening.

Mustafa and Dr. Cramer indicated that they would be following behind us on another boat so that they would be able to see the Maiden's tower from a short distance and try to zoom in on the kidnappers.

We all found two boats waiting for us and the captain, a Turkish nationalist, said that he had been waiting for us and that a woman had been taken over to the island ahead of us. That had to be Ms. Jackson. I asked, but he didn't know for sure. After our brief exchanges, we boarded our boats. The ride would be less than ten minutes, and I looked at Kevin and could see his stress level rising. I had known Kevin for many years, and he and I had been in a lot of difficult situations and yet somehow always survived. My gut feeling told me that this would be no different.

The boat captain slowly steered his boat to the island. We could see the dock approaching, and it looked like Ms. Jackson was there waiting for us. I was greatly relieved, and I suddenly felt a sense of calmness that all would work out. Within a manner of minutes, our boat was at the dock, and the boat hands were securing the robes to the dock. Ms. Jackson saw us and called out, "Hello, my people," which seemed like a strange thing for her to say since she to me had always been a bit aloof.

We all responded back in unison, "Great to see you."

Mustafa and Dr. Cramer were riding in a boat that was a few yards behind us. Kevin and I stepped onto the dock, and we were greeted by Ms. Jackson.

She seemed a bit apprehensive, and I attributed it to that we were headed into unknown territory and that we were not even sure what we were looking for. Our instructions were to offer a blood sacrifice and to make our way to the entrance to the tower, and we would receive further instructions, and we would be reunited with the kidnaped employees and receive the Emerald Dagger.

I somehow wondered if we were walking into a trap or into something that would take us all on another adventure. We spotted the entrance and could see no one around. As we got closer, there was a note taped to one of the doors leading into the tower. It simply said, "Since you have not given us a blood sacrifice, we will have to take matters into our own hands." We all three looked around, and I heard my phone ringing. Most likely Mustafa was texting me from where he was on the boat and had a great view of the tower and the surrounding area. I picked up my phone looked at the text. In bold letters, it read, "GET THE HELL AWAY FROM THERE." I tried to warn Kevin and Ms. Jackson, but at the same time three shots rang out, and suddenly Ms. Jackson dropped to the ground. It appeared that she had been shot in the chest and her body was quickly reacting by shutting down. I grabbed her hand, and she responded by saying, "Check the hotel." She kept saying that repeatedly. I could tell that she was going quickly, and it appeared that there was nothing that Kevin and I could do. I looked up from where I was kneeling and saw someone with a mask on coming toward Kevin and me. A bag was placed over my head, and I felt and heard a crack. I really don't remember what happened next. I heard Mustafa's voice calling my name, and I opened my eyes to find myself lying in a bed. Mustafa told me that I had almost been killed. Kevin was nowhere to be found, and Ms. Jackson was dead. We had no kidnapped employees, nor did we have the famous Emerald Dagger. I closed my eyes and fell fast asleep.

CHAPTER 12

THE CLUES

I woke up with a pounding headache and felt as if time had stood still. I thought back over what had happened. How did I get from the tower area back to my room in the hotel, and how had I avoided being shot? I remembered receiving Mustafa's note and the gunshots. Somewhere in all the commotion, there must be a clue. Who knew we were meeting, and why was Ms. Jackson targeted? What were her last words? Oh yeah. "It's at the hotel. Check the hotel." Check the hotel. Which hotel? What an odd thing to say, yet it must mean something.

Just then I heard a knock on my door. I responded, "Who is it?" The door quickly opened, and there was Mustafa. He made his way into the room, took one look, and begin to speak. He was interrupted with another knock. In walked Dr. Reverend Sterling Holt. He asked how I was feeling and then offered his perspective as to what had occurred.

He said, "I saw two individuals that were dressed in brown robes with hoods on, and they were in Mandarin Tower when you, Inspector, were approaching it. The two hooded individuals seemed like they were familiar with the place and seemed to know where they were going."

I looked up, and into my room came Jerry Davison. He looked upset and was holding a piece of paper in his hand. He thrust out his hand to me and said, "Read this." I took the note from his hand and began to read, "Dear

Inspector, our deal was for you to provide a blood sacrifice for exchange for release of the kidnapped employees and the dagger. Since you provided no blood sacrifice, we took it into our hands to provide one. Ms. Jackson is our blood sacrifice."

I turned to Mr. Davison and asked how he obtained the note. He said a woman or a man (he wasn't sure) dressed in a brown robe delivered it to the front desk and asked that it be given to the hotel manager. "Sally, my front desk manager, did not ask any more of the person and informed me when I arrived that someone in a monk-type robe had left a note for me."

I sat up and bed and looked at the group that had surrounded my bed and said, "Be careful with everywhere you go and who you talk with. Our every move is being watched by someone or something."

One by one the group began to leave. I turned to Mustafa and asked if he could stay for a few minutes. I needed to think. On their way out we all agreed to meet later that day at 5:00 p.m. at the hotel bar. Mustafa watched them leave and turned to me and asked, "Do you need anything, Inspector?"

I responded, "Yes, some answers."

Mustafa looked at me with that all too familiar look that said, "Do you want me to help you to figure this out?" Mustafa and I together than reviewed the events that he witnessed from his vantage point. Mustafa said, "Dr. Reverend Holt and I made our way to the top of the tower, and when we made our way to the balcony, that gave us a clear view of the area surrounding the tower and a partial view of the area below the tower. Within a few minutes after you left, Inspector, Dr. Reverend Holt and I began to see what appeared to be a small boat craft, and we watched them tie up the boat to the dock behind the tower.

"We clearly saw four individuals all dressed in brown monk like robes make their way to the side entrance on the tower. One appeared to be carrying what looked like a gun. That is when I texted you, Inspector, and told you to get the hell out of there because you were walking right into their path, and you had no idea what you were walking into.

"We saw Ms. Jackson fall, and that is when we got out of where we were at and quickly ran down the stairs from the inside of the tower and made ourselves through the opposite tower door to you. I witnessed a person in a brown robe stroke you over the head and put a bag over your head. When Dr.

CHAPTER 12

Holt and I arrived, the four robed figures dropped you and ran to where their boat was docked and tied up. We turned to go after them, but they knew the terrain, and we watched as they quickly got onto their boat and sped away. One of them appeared to be a woman, but I wasn't completely sure because all were wearing those brown monk-like robes."

Mustafa looked at me and said, "I believe that I know who one of the four was."

I replied, "Oh, really?"

"Yes." He then went on to say, "About two weeks ago I was visiting with Mr. Davison at the hotel, and I saw a woman that I thought I recognized but couldn't place here name or from where I knew her from. Then it dawned on me. I had waited on her at the Grand Hotel in Nephi, USA, where I was working for Mr. Davison. It was the Reverend Janice Turner. She was in the hotel meeting with Ms. Jackson, and at the time, I really didn't think anything about it, but now I wonder why she was here meeting with Ms. Jackson."

I looked at Mustafa and said, "Ms. Jackson had told me in a conversation that Revered Janice and Reverend Austin were both here in Istanbul staying at the Hotel Sultan. I went to their hotel and visited with Reverend Turner and Reverend Austin and asked them why they were here. She told me that they were here doing research on Otman artifacts. At the time I thought it was a bit odd, but then I remembered that Reverend Turner before ministry had worked for an international marketing company, and Reverend Roper had worked for the State Department as a peace corps worker and later a Middle Eastern attaché. Interesting they both had a connection to Ms. Jackson."

I thought of Ms. Jackson's last words, "Check the hotel." I shared this with Mustafa, and he said, "Have you done that?"

"No." And I said, "I wonder what hotel she was referring to." Mustafa suggested that we first start with the hotel that we both are staying at and ask Mr. Davison if he can let us into Ms. Jackson's room. Mustafa helped me out of my bed and helped me make my way to my hotel room door.

"Mustafa," I said, "can you call Mr. Davison and tell him to meet me in the lobby?"

"Sure thing, Inspector."

We both made our way to the elevator, and we both knew that somewhere we were going to find the clues that would begin to tie a lot of the case together. Mustafa and I had been through a lot. He had helped me in my last case by supplying me with information he observed while performing his job as a bartender. In his new job, he worked for the American Embassy as an interpreter and as a liaison between Americans working and living in Istanbul who were there on short term visas. His specialty was Arabic languages, and he had been in contact with Dr. Reverend Michael Cramer, Dr. Reverend Sterling Holt, and recently with Reverends Turner and Roper.

Mustafa and I had a special relationship where we both looked out for each other. Mustafa had acted as interpreter when we were meeting those strangers at the Blue Mosque. Mustafa turned to me and said, "Inspector, I believe I know who is behind these happenings, and I think I know a way in which we can prove it."

My eyes lit up, and I said, "Mustafa, what is your plan?"

He went on to say, as the elevator doors were opening, "Reverend Turner and Reverend Roper are involved. When they came to meet with me, they were interested in finding out what I knew about the famous Emerald Dagger and about the art theft and fake replacements of Turkish art by a team of professional thieves.

"At the time they said they were working as a team in connection with the Turkish government to write about the theft and the famous Emerald Dagger. They were here on professional writers' visas, and that gave them access to many of the government documents about the theft and the replacement of much of the original art with forgeries. I thought it was strange at the time. Why would two reverends be so interested in Turkish art and artifacts from the Ottoman Empire. To do that type of research in Turkey, the government requires a sponsor. The sponsor was listed as ORT, Ottoman Research and Technology, which I later learned was owned by Kevin Hanes and Ms. Elizabeth Jackson."

The doors to the elevator opened, and we both stepped into the lobby. I turned to Mustafa. "We need to find Mr. Davison to get his key and permission to be let into Ms. Jackson's room." I looked across the lobby and saw that Mr. Davison was making his way toward both Mustafa and me in what appeared to be in a harried fashion.

CHAPTER 12

Mr. Davison called out, "Inspector, so glad to see you. I hear that you have been looking for me. How can I assist you?"

Without stopping I blurted out, "Can you come with us and open Ms. Jackson's room?"

"Very well, Inspector, let's go."

We made our way to the elevator, it opened, and we all stepped in. Mr. Davison pushed the button for the top floor.

The elevator stopped, and the doors opened, and we all made our way to Ms. Jackson's room. It was in the middle of the hallway, and Mr. Davison arrived first and took out his pass key card and quickly opened the room door. Mustafa and I pushed our way into the room and began to survey the room with our detailed eyes. Mr. Davison excused himself and left Mustafa and me in the room. Mustafa started checking out the closet while I looked around the bed, the nightstand, and the dresser top.

Nothing appeared to be out of order. That seemed strange to me because Ms. Jackson in my past interventions appeared not to be all that organized. It was as if the room had been staged. We were about to give up when I thought to look inside one of the pillows. Stuffed into the pillow was a small envelope, and in that envelope was a key. The key looked to be the type of key to a safe deposit box or a locker. Mustafa also found that in the bottom of one of the dresser drawers was a diagram of the Median Tower along with the boat schedules for the ferry that came to the island. Both clues were not much, but they did give us something to move forward on. I couldn't help but feel that there had been more in the room, but someone had gotten there before us and removed an item or items.

We had a key, and now we had to figure out what the key went to, a safe deposit box or locker. Either way it was a great clue, and Mustafa and I would have to follow it through to see where it would lead us. It appeared to me as I started to ponder over this case. "Whom can I trust? Kevin was now a possible suspect, Mr. Davison, Dr. Holt, Dr. Cramer, Reverends Turner and Roper. The only person I can trust is Mustafa. He has nothing to gain in all of this, yet he has connections with all the parties."

I turned to Mustafa and said, "Let's go. We are done here." Mustafa walked toward the open door, and I followed close behind. On the way out I shut the door, turned to Mustafa, and said, "You, my good friend, are the only person I can trust." I went on to say, "I need your help on this case, and let's continue to work together. You have connections with all the possible suspects as well as the Turkish government.

Mustafa smiled and said, "Let's solve this case."

CHAPTER 13
MORE CLUES

Mustafa and I made our way to the elevator we needed to find out just what the key we found opened. It looked like a safe deposit box or a locker key. The elevator opened, and we both got in and noticed a strange man looking at us. Mustafa said to him in Arabic, "Good day, brother."

He responded back, "Be careful."

I asked Mustafa if he knew the man. He responded that he was one of the Turkish secret police that he had connected with when he arrived in Istanbul. They work independently from the government but provide a service for foreign nationals. He had introduced Ms. Jackson to them a few months ago when she arrived in Istanbul. She wanted to find out about the art thefts from several years ago and all about the Ottoman artifacts, particularly the Emerald Dagger.

Mustafa went on further to tell me that at the time he didn't think much of Ms. Jackson's request because she was investing in a Turkish start-up company, and she had just purchased the hotel, and he considered her requests as more informational, given her background in business. Ms. Jackson had met with Reverends Austin and Janice in the hotel on several occasions. Mustafa said, "Inspector, at the time I saw them meeting, and I thought I had recognized Reverends Janice and Austin, but I wasn't sure, so I just didn't think about their meeting until when you arrived, and things started happening."

"Interesting," I said. "So, from what you are telling me, Ms. Jackson knew all along that Reverend Janice Turner and the Reverend Austin Roper were here, and the three of them had to be planning something. Ms. Jackson is all about money and opportunity, and I bet that the other two are looking for ways to make a fast buck."

"What was it that all of them were after and why did all three not be 100 percent honest with me? What are they trying to hide? What is the connection with Kevin and his employees and his company and all the happenings with the art theft, the Emerald Dagger, and the kidnapped employees?"

Mustafa turned to me and said, "Give me the key, and I am going to ask at the front desk if this is a key to their safe deposit boxes." He left me standing, and I watched as he made his way across the lobby to the front desk, which was in the far corner just opposite the bar. I found my way to one of the overstuffed chairs in the middle of the lobby sat down and tried to take in all that had happened. I could see Mustafa talking to the front desk clerk, and it looked like she was telling him something that put what looked like a smile on his face. Mustafa looked over and caught my eye and he gave me a thumbs-up as he walked over to where I was sitting.

When he arrived, he said, "The key goes to a locker at the Hotel Sultan, and if I remember, that is the hotel where Reverend Janice Turner and Reverend Austin Roper are staying.

"Interesting," I replied. "Let's go over and check this out." Mustafa helped me up, and we turned toward the door. Just as we started to walk to the exit of the hotel, Mr. Jerry Davison appeared, and he was walking toward us, and he appeared to be very upset.

Just then, Mr. Davison called out, "Inspector Sterling, I need to talk with you."

I waved to indicate that I had heard him and turned to Mustafa and said, "I wonder what he wants."

Within seconds, Mr. Davison was standing right in front of both of us. He said in a very loud, angry voice, "I understand that you found a key in Ms. Jackson's room. Why didn't you come to me to ask about it?"

"Well," I said "because—"

Mustafa chimed in. "Because we didn't want to bother you with everything else that has happened and the fact that you lost both your business

CHAPTER 13

partner, Ms. Jackson, and your new vice president of finance, Ms. Nancy. You are dealing with a lot. We learned from your front desk employee that the key is for a locker in the Hotel Sultan. In fact, that is where Inspector Sterling and I are headed; you are welcome to join us.

"No, that's OK, but in the future anything that happens in this hotel let me be the first to know about it."

"We can do that, "Mustafa responded. We wished Mr. Jerry Davison a cheerful goodbye, walked out the door of the hotel, and turned right to make the walk to the Hotel Sultan. I had walked it previously, and I knew the way. Mustafa followed a close step behind.

The Hotel Sultan was about a five-minute walk away. As we walked, I could see the Blue Mosque off to our right, and far off in the distance was the Maiden's Tower. I wondered what treasures we would find in the locker. Mustafa shouted for me to look to my immediate left, As I turned, I saw what appeared to be a man in a black suit, and he was walking in a quick pace to ward what appeared to be the Hotel Sultan. Mustafa said, "He is one of the secret Turkey plain-clothed policemen." Mustafa went further onto explain that when he arrived in Istanbul several months ago, he was briefed by this group and informed that they have reason to believe that the missing manuscripts, artifacts, and paintings that were stolen from the Palace Museum were being stored somewhere here in Istanbul.

Mustafa further went onto explain that he witnessed a meeting with the secret police and Ms. Johnson about a week ago at the Hotel Sultan. I motioned to Mustafa that we needed to cross the street because we were in front of the Hotel Sultan. We waited until it was clear and then both made our way across the street. We both paused in front of the hotel doors and waited for the doorman to welcome us and to open the doors. I greeted him by saying, "Hello, Omar." He had his name proudly displayed on his uniform, which was a bright-red jacket with brass buttons that opened down his front. Wrapped around his waist was a sash that had gold brocade around its edges and a dark fabric inside. Omar opened the door, and Mustafa and I entered. Mustafa took the lead and found the front desk. He recognized one of the employees and started conversing with him in Arabic. I stood there in amazement and feeling very appreciative that I had Mustafa with me. After a few moments Mustafa turned around and said to me, "Inspector, Emmad here will take us to the lockers and confirmed that the key we found is from their hotel lockers."

Emmad lead the way, which was only fitting since his name means "leader," and Mustafa and I followed close behind. He took us through the lobby through a gold door in the corner and down a narrow hallway. We stopped at another set of double doors, and Emmad opened them. We walked through into a large room that had lockers on all four sides with a small round coach type in the middle of the room. Emmad said, "Your locker is the large one over there in the far-right corner." We walked toward the locker. The door itself was about the size of a regular door to a room and the locker went from the floor to the ceiling, which was about seven feet high. We matched the key, number 704, with the locker number, and Mustafa put the key into the lock. He gave it a quick turn to the right and heard the lock click.

I carefully approached the locker with a sense of anticipation. As Mustafa opened the locker, much to my surprise, we both stood there and staired into the open locker. There was a series of about five shelves, which were about four to five feet deep. The shelves had all sorts of items and things on them. Emmad commented, "Ya Allah," which translates to "Oh God." Before our eyes we could see what appeared to be several ancient manuscripts, each carefully wrapped in protective material. Mustafa exclaimed, "These manuscripts are centuries old, and I bet that they contain historical texts that are both invaluable and irreplaceable." We then saw numerous pieces of artwork, including paintings and sculptures, all meticulously crafted to resemble famous originals. Some were half finished, revealing the process of their creation, with sketches and reference images pinned to the interior of the locker door. A collection of artifacts from the Ottoman era, including intricately designed ceramics, jewelry, and textiles. Each item was labeled with its historical significance and origin, some still bearing evidence of hasty removal from their original locations.

A folder filled with documents that appeared to detail the operations of a crime ring. Among these papers were lists of individuals involved in the crimes, including the masterminds behind the thefts, forgers of the art, and smugglers of the artifacts. The names included not only the criminals but also contacts and accomplices in various parts of the world.

CHAPTER 13

A series of photographs depicting the stolen items in their original settings, surveillance photos of the criminals, and maps with marked locations of previous heists and planned future targets.

Detailed ledgers showing the financial transactions involved in the illegal operations. These records included payments to various individuals, sales records of stolen or forged items, and laundering of money through different channels.

I turned to Mustaf and his new friend Emmad and remarked, "The contents of this locker not only confirm the involvement of the individuals we have been investigating but also provide an overview of a crime ring's operations that others had talked about but were never able to prove. I am sure as I study these documents I will find the names of Reverend Austin Roper, Reverend Janice Turner, Ms. Elizabeth Johnson, Dr. Cramer, and Reverend Dr. Sterling Holt."

I still needed to figure out how Kevin and his employees play into it or if they do at all. In addition, what did Nancy know and why was she killed? And why was Ms. Jackson killed? Going all the way back to the first murder at the Munich airport being Selim. "I bet," I thought to myself, "many of the answers to these questions lie in these detailed documents. I can understand now why Ms. Jackson's last words were, 'Check the hotel." she wanted me to find this."

I turned to Emmad and Mustafa and said, "Mustafa, can you contact the Turkish secret police? And Emmad, can you inform your boss that we will be back? And don't let your two guests Reverend Austin Roper and Reverend Janice Turner check out of the hotel without first informing myself or Mustafa."

I needed time to think and to process all the treasure trove of information that we had found. Mustafa, I said, "Can you bring the box of detailed ledgers with you? And let's go back to the hotel and check in with Kevin and Mr. Jerry Davison. Let's not tell them anything about this until we have had a chance to go over it and contact the Turkish secret police." Mustafa carefully put the items back in the locker and kept the box of detailed legers out, put the key in the locker, and locked it back up and walked out of the room and down the hall and across the lobby, through the front doors, and into the street. We needed to take a break at our hotel and started walking back.

CHAPTER 14
MORE ANSWERS

Mustafa and I made our way back to our hotel. Mustafa carried the boxes of ledgers, and I went over and over in my mind all the facts that we had learned from what we found in the locker. It was apparent to both of us that we needed to bring in some help, and that would mean involving the Turkish secret police. Something that I did not want to do until I had it clear in my mind just how all the pieces fit together.

Mustafa and I didn't say a word to each other on our short walk back to the hotel. Once we arrived, we walked into the vast lobby, and Mustafa turned to me and said, "Inspector, where to next?"

I suggested, "Why don't we go up to my room and take another look over all the information that we had gleaned from the ledgers?"

We both made our way to the elevators. Once inside Mustafa broke our silence by saying, "Inspector, I think we need to contract the Turkish secret police." I nodded in agreement to him. The elevator rose and soon we were on my floor. The door opened, and out we stepped and started walking to the left and down the long hallway where my suite was located at the end. Once we arrived, Mustafa opened the door with my pass card, and he walked in, and I followed. On the far end of my suite was a small room where a large table was, and I said to Mustafa, "Let's lay the records out on the table and see what more we discover."

CHAPTER 14

I remembered back reading in one of the files that Kevin had sent me, about the art theft in Turkey in 2008. The famous art theft in Turkey in 2008 involved the theft of valuable paintings from the State Art and Sculpture Museum in Ankara. The theft occurred in March 2008. The thieves stole eight paintings by renowned Turkish artists, including works by Hoca Ali Riza, Nuri Iyem, and others. In total experts had put the theft of over 302 paintings. It was later discovered in 2012 that 46 of the works of art that had been stolen were replaced by fakes.

Further on in that same file, I learned that it had been an organized crime syndicate that had been responsible for the art thefts. An arrest was made by an anonymous phone call made to the Turkish culture minister at the time. The caller, said to be an antiques dealer referred to himself as the pseudonym, "Daylight," daylight was able to revel extensive details about the operation. His identity to this day has never been confirmed.

According to "Daylight," the group of criminals brought forgers from Ukraine's Aivazovsky Painting Academy into Turkey to produce the fakes they eventually swapped for the museum's originals. "Daylight" said that after the originals were removed from the museum, the group "sold them to famous businessmen through mediators and antique dealers known in their fields."

According to a police report by in 2012, claimed several of the stolen works had been recovered but the vast majority remain unaccounted for, and fifteen individuals were identified as being involved but only three were brought to justice. The others, along with many of the art and artifacts, were still out there.

Recalling the files that Kevin had sent me to read over, I was struck that this person named Daylight was never identified. Yet he was the one who cracked open the case for the secret Turkish police. I also was interested if in the ledgers that the names and the transactions for the art that was stolen and the art that was forged are identified. I also would like to see if there is a connection between Ms. Elizabeth Jackson, Reverend Janice Turner, Reverend Austin Roper, and Selim.

Mustafa reminded me that this information is a big help, but we still haven't solved the murders or found the missing employees. "Mustafa, "I said, "we are getting closer. I feel it. I needed to have a discussion with Kevin and at least let Jerry Davison, the hotel manager, know that we are getting closer to solving the case." Mustafa said his goodbyes and left to do some inquiries with his contacts at the Turkish secret police. I said goodbye and watched him leave. When the door shut, I sat down in one of the larger cushion chairs and just took in a breath and paused.

Somewhere in all the ledgers that we had uncovered lay many of the answers I was seeking. One of the rules in Investigating is, "Follow the money." It will always lead you to those who are in the know. I thought of Nancy, who had been killed. How tragic for her. She must have found out something with ether the hotel finances and records or with Kevin's financial records. Nancy from my past working relationship was sharp, and she knew her stuff, and she was a great auditor.

Which reminds me: In all the excitement over her death and meeting the kidnappers and Ms. Johnson's murder, Mustafa and I had failed to check out Nancy's hotel room to see if she had any information that might be useful to our investigation. She was hired by Ms. Jackson and Kevin to review financial records. I wonder what she found out that could have caused her to be murdered. Many questions to solve and with each answer another question.

I sat down at my table and opened the first ledger marked, "Operation Izmir." As I opened the ledger my eyes were drawn right away to the organized detail that they had gone to pull off the thefts. On the paper in front of me, the criminals had clearly defined how they would carry out the art thefts. Someone had indicated that they would need inside connections that could provide the critical information about security measures, the layout of the museum, and locations of valuable items. On the following pages were detailed reports on the layout of the security, weak points, the museum's schedule, and the routines of the security personnel as well as the positioning of the security cameras.

There was another page all about fake documents and disguises, copies of forged documents to gain access to restricted areas. Also, information on how to pose as a museum staff, contractor, or researcher so that one could move around the museum without arousing suspicion. Further on in the ledger was a page labeled "High-Tech Tools." This outlined sophisticated tools and technology to use to bypass security systems. There were instructions on disabling alarm systems, hacking into security networks, and using specialized equipment to break into display cases without setting off alarms.

CHAPTER 14

It became very clear to me that this operation was a coordinated effort, and that the thieves knew what they were doing and had set up a whole network for smuggling contacts and smuggling routes. And there in the middle of the page in bold lettering appeared the name of Ms. Elizabeth Jackson. She was listed as the operation consultant but also listed in the document as someone to contact who was very active in the network. Close by her names in bold letters were the names of other consultants, Janice Turner, Austin Roper, Ahmet Yilmaz, who was the current vice president of Hao Technologies.

Potential buyers were listed on another page. There one name that stuck out was Mr. Jerry Davison along with Asel Ozturk and Richard Franklin who are current employees of Kevin's company Hao Technologies. Other possible buyers were listed as: Reverend Michael Cramer, Dr. Reverend Sterling Halt. In one way or another people in my group were connected, either in the theft of the art and artifacts or in the selling and purchasing.

I had to meet with Reverends Janice Turner and Reverend Austin Roper. They had some explaining to do to me and I needed to hear from them just how they got involved in this operation. Apparently, this Operation Izmir is still somewhat active. The art, the manuscripts, and the Emerald Dagger are all connected. Three murders along with the kidnapped employees and now a treasure trove of information and items. My task as I see it is to figure out the different roles that each of the players played and why some of them lost their life because of the role that they played or didn't play. No wonder Kevin called me and asked me to take this case.

I feel like I am missing a clue, and I hope that by searching Nancy's room that I might find something. I put a call into Mustafa to see how his meeting went with his contact in the Turkish secret police. I texted him and asked him to meet me in the lobby of the hotel. He texted me back and said he would be there in about ten minutes. That gave me time to get down to the lobby and stop off as well to see Mr. Jerry Davison, if he was in his office.

I walked out of my room and down the hall toward the elevator, pushed the button, and the door open almost immediately. I got in and pressed the L for lobby, and quickly the elevator descended to the lobby level. There was one ding, and the doors opened. I stepped forward and moved quickly out into the lobby. Far in the opposite corner was where the front desk was and behind that Mr. Davison's office. I made my way there, and much to my delight Mr. Davison was standing in front of the main desk conversing with a hotel guest. He saw me coming toward him, and before I could greet him, he greeted me. "Inspector Sterling, how are you doing today?"

We both exchanged niceties, and then I asked him if he could let me into Nancy's room. He picked up his master key card, and away we both went back across the lobby to the bank of elevators. We arrived just in time to catch one that was headed up to the fourth floor. I heard the ding of the elevator telling us that we had arrived at the fourth floor. Mr. Davison and I got out quickly and turned to the right and then a quick left, and about halfway down in the middle on the left-hand side was Nancy's room, room number 435.

Mr. Davison let me into the room by him using his key card. Once inside he turned to me and said, "I will leave you here, and if you need anything else, please ask." With that he turned and went back through the door. I looked around, and it looked just the way I had imagined Nancy's room would look. Papers were neatly stacked on the desk. Clothes hung up in the closet and shoes neatly paired on the floor of the closet. On the desk I noticed two file folders that appeared to contain a lot of paper. One was over an inch thick and the other very thin, maybe an inch.

I knew Nancy when she worked for the Interim Ministry Network, and she was director of finance, and she kept very detailed financial records. She had told me on the plane that she was hired by Ms. Jackson to be the vice president of finance and was hired by Kevin, my friend, as a contractor to review his company's books and financial information. I was hoping that I would find in Nancy's detailed records a possible reason why she was murdered. I had my work cut out for me, but I was hopeful that the spirit of Nancy would lead and guide me to the answers that I was seeking.

CHAPTER 15

NANCY'S INFORMATION

I sat at Nancy's desk and opened the larger file first. That file was of the expenses at the hotel. Much of it was a series of excel spreadsheets with columns and numbers, but Nancy had noted out to the side things that appeared to be odd and items that she needed to ask ether Kevin or Jerry Davison about. The first notation was an expense paid out Hao Technologies for $50,000, which was noted for services rendered. I knew that this was my friend Kevin's company and that part of what they did was specialize in cataloging and selling ancient works of art. I am sure that Nancy wanted to know what type of services the hotel hired Kevin's company for. I also would like to know.

I came to another page and there was another notation again on the expense of $150,000 paid to Ms. Elizabeth Jackson for rare art. She was an investor in the hotel Nancy had noted to ask Ms. Jackson about this. On another expense page $250,000 for Operation Izmir was circled and Nancy had noted what is this company? I continued to review the financial records and learned that Mr. Jerry Davison had set up whole separate accounting ledgers for Hao Technologies and that he and Ms. Jackson had invested each a half of million dollars and were major stockholders in Kevins company.

I next opened the next file, and it was called Operation Izmir. Nancy had found an organizational chart that included as main consultants Dr. Reverend Sterling Halt, Reverend Michael Cramer, Reverend Austin Roper,

Reverend Janice Turner, and Ms. Elizabeth Jackson. As lead consultant was listed Ahmet Yilmaz, I recognized his name as being the vice president of operations for Hao Technologies' and one of the three employees who had been kidnapped and had had his throat slashed. Noted off to the side was the name Selim Aksu with a side note: An investor in the Hotel Miughaamara. I had forgotten that he and Ahmet had invested in the hotel along with Ms. Jackson and Mr. Jerry Davison.

For the first time since I started on investigating this case, things started to make sense. I would need to spend more time with Mustafa in going over all the information that we found in the locker, but parts of the story are beginning to fall into place. I now had the proof as to why this whole cast of characters were here in Istanbul. Mustafa and I had our work cut out for us. We now need to take an inventory with all the art pieces that we found in the locker and compare them against any insurance claims reports and who in those claims received the payoffs.

We also needed to look at the estimated values of the art and artifacts and see if there were any businesses that reflected the stolen items as losses. The great thing is that because of Mustafa's connection with the Turkish secret police, they had been working on this case of Operation Izmir for years and their information with the information and items that we have found should provide Mustafa and I with a clear path of where the money was passed, who benefited, and who might have had reason and motive to even commit murder to save their reputation or their name or their business. The thread of deceit and murder were starting to unravel. I wasn't sure yet who was behind the murders and the kidnapping of Kevin's employees, but I was beginning to get a clearer picture of who that might be.

I called Mustafa and asked me if he could meet me in my room in about an hour. I said, "I have some new information to share with you about the case." He responded that he also had been talking with his contacts in the Turkish secret police and that they had provided him with a lot of information even some new leads on where the two remaining employees of Kevin's company might be being held.

What a day it had been. Little did I ever imagine that a key found in a pillow would lead Mustafa and me to a treasure full of such vast stolen art pieces and the records to document most of the key parties that have been

CHAPTER 15

and were involved with Operation Izmir. I had to meet with Kevin and really have a heart-to-heart talk with him and tell him what I had found and try to get his response about all of this. He had been a police investigator, and he had worked with me in the past so he because of our relationship would tell me the truth. I knew Kevin and I knew that all of this had taken a toll on him. He hadn't said much about his employees, but the murders of Nancy, Selim, and Ms. Jackson must be upsetting to him. Yet according to what I am discovering from what Nancy had uncovered, Kevin or his company was involved in this Operation Izmir.

Then what about Mr. Jerry Davison? He invested in the hotel that he is now the general manger of, the Hotel Miughaamara, and Ms. Jackson was also an investor. I believe that Mustafa and I need to have a real discussion with Jerry to find out what does he know and share with him a portion of what we have discovered. I have dealt with Jerry before and found him to be a very smart businessman and someone who was smart when it came to investing.

Jerry had given me access to Nancy's room, so I am sure he is wondering what, if anything, I found out. I looked at my watch; it was getting close to five thirty, and I told Mustafa that I would meet him in an hour and a half hour had already gone by. It was time for me to stop by the front desk and see if I could catch Mr. Davison and then go to my room to meet Mustafa. I got up from Nancys desk and took one last look around the room and was ready to walk out when out of the corner of my eye something caught my attention. I turned and stared right at the coffee maker. At first glance everything about it looked normal, but then I saw what my eye had caught slightly sticking out of the top where one would pour in the water was a small piece of paper. I fetched it and unrolled it. Written on the paper were the words, "Help us B224." I had no idea what this could mean, but the fact that Nancy must have received this note, or somehow acquired it and perhaps she could find out what, where and so forth. She was murdered.

My inspector sense told me that this note was important and perhaps even a clue. Who wrote it, where was B224, and was it for real? "Oh, Nancy, I wish you were here so you could tell me." I picked up the note and put it into my pocket and filed it away in my mind that here was another thing to discuss with Mustafa. I stopped and thought and pondered but now had no idea. I waked toward the hotel door opened it and walked out into the hallway. I would stop by the front desk first to see if Mr. Davison is in than go to my room and wait for Mustafa to arrive.

I took the elevator down to the lobby walked out and turned to my right. I walked across the vast lobby over to the front desk area. As I approached Mr. Davison appeared to be in a heated discussion with one of his employees, Martha Wong, the head of housekeeping. By the expression on her face, she was not happy by what Mr. Davison was telling her. I could not hear what was being said, but it apparently was one of those discussion where the boss is not pleased with their employee. As I approached Mr. Davison saw me and said, "Inspector, how are you? Did you finish with Nancy's room?" I said yes and thanked him and then asked hm if he and I could meet tomorrow morning for me to give him an update. We agreed on 9:00 a.m. He walked away, and I turned to walk back to the elevator and go back to my room.

I thought, "I wonder if I ask Ms. Wong if she had ever heard about B224." I yelled out, "Ms. Wong. "She quickly turned around to see where the sound of her name was coming from, and I, at the same time, motioned with my hands for her to come to me. She came over, and I asked her if she had even heard about B224. At first, she looked puzzled, and I asked, "What's wrong?"

Ms. Wong responded in a somewhat broken English, "That number corresponds to a set of rooms that we no longer use here at the hotel. They are in a remote part of the basement, and during the remodeling were mostly cut off from the rest of the remodeled hotel."

"Could I see them?" I asked.

She said, "No, only Mr. Davison is the only one who is allowed in that area of the hotel."

I thanked her for her information and said, "Can you keep this discussion just between us?"

She smiled and nodded and said yes, and off she went. I stood there for a moment and pondered over the information that I had been given. I turned toward the elevator waited for it to arrive. When it did, I stepped in and pushed the button 4 and waited for the elevator to rise. Within no time, it stopped, opened, and it was my floor. I stepped out and walked toward my room.

CHAPTER 16
ANOTHER EXCITING ADVENTURE

I arrived at my door to my room, paused for a moment and thought about Ms. Wong's words: "It's a part of the hotel that is cut off, and we don't use it anymore. Mr. Davidson has the only key." Why would Nancy have a piece of paper with the words "Help us, B224"? I needed to talk with Mr. Davison. But somehow, I needed to do so without him knowing that I knew about B224. Mustafa had lots of experience in asking questions to obtain information without having the person know the reason why you are asking the question. Mustafa had learned the art of doing this because of his work with the embassy and dealing with Middle Eastern Turkish nationalists. I heard a ding on my phone indicating that I had just received a text. It was from Mustafa; he was telling me that he was on his way up.

I took a deep breath and paused. Answers seemed to be coming now in waves, and I believe I am getting closer to solving this complex set of murders. With Mustafa's assistance I am sure that we will both figure this out. Just then I heard a knock on my door. I opened it, and there was Mustafa. He looked happy and eager to begin to problem-solve. He walked in and set down on the bed and begin to talk. His discussions with the Turkish secret police yielded a lot of information. He learned that the group Operation Izar had been actively trading for the past several years, and each time the Turkish secret police were getting ready to close in on them, things changed, and their operation seemed to go underground. It was as if they had an informant that seemed to know what the secret police had and when they were going to strike and make some arrests. Mustafa seemed to think that the mole in the Turkish police was Reverend Cramer. Before ministry he worked for the FBI in Middle Eastern operations. In fact, some of the first thefts back in 2008 occurred during the time that he was serving in the Turkish office as a specialist in Ottoman Empire artifacts and Turkish ancient manuscripts.

Mustafa believed that the Reverend Cramer had a behind-the-scenes understanding with the Turkish secret police that he would report anything that he saw, and they would do the same for him. We both knew that his name was on the documents listing the leaders in the organization. So Reverend Cramer must be playing both sides of the fence, so to speak. He was now more than a person of interest. I explained to Mustafa that while searching in Nancy's room, I found a small piece of paper by the coffee station that said, "Help us B224."

Reverend Cramer might even know the history of the hotel where we were staying and if he could remember ever being in an area that could be considered a basement level. Mustafa spoke up and said, "I can request from the secret police for some blueprints before the remodeling in 2016."

"That would help us to get a good idea about the hotel," I said. Mustafa reminded me that we were still looking for the Emerald Dagger as well as the kidnapped employees from Kevin's company. We were closing in and yet still lots of unanswered questions, and I was beginning to see that Mustafa was really the only one I could trust in helping me to solve these murders and the theft of the Emerald Dagger and find the kidnapped employees.

I looked at Mustafa. What a real lifesaver he had been to this whole case. In my last case, the Case of the Wondering Minister, Mustafa had provided needed information that led me to the killer. He wasn't so much providing me with the information as to using his contacts in Turkey to assist us in solving the case. Mustafa's understanding of Arabic and his connections with the Turkish secret police were coming in very handy.

Mustafa said, "What next, Inspector?" I heard his question but didn't respond right away. I thought back to past experiences here in Istanbul. Who killed Selim in Munich? Who knew I was on a flight with Nancy to Istanbul and placed the note with the package in the airplane's bathroom?

CHAPTER 16

Who arranged for us to meet with the Turkish religious leaders (I think) or whatever they were in the Blue Mosque after afternoon prayer services? Who arranged for Ms. Jackson and Reverend Cramer, and Reverend Dr. Stan Holt to go to the Maiden's Tower to meet with the kidnappers and exchange and receive the Emerald Dagger? Someone or more than one oversaw this operation and controlled it and always seemed to be one step ahead of us except for finding the key in Nancy's room.

I responded finally to Mustafa by saying, "Whoever was behind all of this was very clever, and I am not sure what their reasons are, but it all must be tied to the stolen art, artifacts, and of course perhaps even the legend of the Emerald Dagger." I then went on to share with Mustafa what I knew about the legend of the Emerald Dagger. The legend of the Emerald Dagger is a fascinating tale combining history, myth, and intrigue. The dagger is said to have originated from the Topkapi Palace, the primary residence of the Ottoman sultans for approximately four hundred years.

In the basement of the palace was where the dagger was last on display before it was stolen. It was to be the center piece for the art show of Ottoman art and artifacts. This show, if I remembered, was being sponsored by Kevin's company. Kevin described the dagger to me as being an ornate weapon, encrusted with large emeralds and other precious stones.

Kevin as well as the late Ms. Elizabeth Jackson told me about the legend of the Emerald Dagger.

According to legend, the dagger was commissioned by Sultan Mahmud I (reigned 1730–1754). It was intended as a gift for the Persian ruler Nader Shah. However, Nader Shah was assassinated before the dagger could be delivered, and it remained in the Ottoman treasury. Some versions of the legend say that the dagger is cursed, bringing misfortune to those who possess it. Kevin told me that the dagger has been the subject of numerous stories and myths, murder, and betrayal. It is said that many have sought the dagger, believing it to hold great power or a hidden secret only to have misfortune follow them some even murdered.

Mustafa, after hearing my tale of the Emerald Dagger, responded by saying, "The Emerald Dagger had always been the key to solving this case. Whoever possess it or knows where it is has the power to create murder, myth, and mystery and attribute it to the dagger."

"I agree, Mustafa. Now as far as next steps. Mustafa. I believe that a key to finding he kidnapped employees is tied into this B224 area of rooms in the basement of the hotel. You and I need to find a way to get into that part of the hotel. We need to get in there without drawing suspicion from Mr. Davison. What if the secret police did a raid on the hotel in the name of a tip that was received about the hotel for a place where the kidnapped employees could be being kept? That way Mr. Davison would not expect that you and I were behind the tip. If he is involved, he could possibly lead us to the killer." Mustafa nodded his head as agreement to our plan. We both took that last glance to look each other in the eye, and then Mustafa got up, and I followed. Mustafa said that he was on his way to meet with his contact with the secret police, and I told Mustafa that I needed to connect with Kevin and have an honest discussion with him.

I went onto explain to Mustafa as we both were walking toward the elevator that I had a meeting set up with Mr. Davison tomorrow morning at 9:00 a.m., so that might be a great time to plan the raid shortly after that. The elevator doors opened. We both stepped in and said nothing more on the way down to the lobby. We were both feeling a since of destiny and purpose. We were onto something, and whatever the cost, were determined to see it all the way through. The elevator stopped, the door opened, and we both stepped out and looked at each other and simply said nothing. That look in both of our eyes said volumes. We were both committed to seeing this case through, and we were getting closer to solving it. I went off to look for Kevin, and Mustafa went to have coffee with his secret police contacts.

CHAPTER 17
A CONVERSATION WITH INSPECTOR STERLING

When I came out of the elevator and watched Mustafa leave, I took a moment to pause and to ponder over where we were at in solving this case. There is something in this case that I am not seeing, but somehow, I believe that when I do, I will be able to solve this case. My instincts and my gut feelings and hunches are telling me that Kevin has not been totally up front with me and that he is hiding something. He reached out to me because he knew I would be able to solve this case. But what if he also reached out to me because he knew that in solving the case, I would uncover information that he wanted others to know about but was in a position that he could not disclose for fear of losing his own life?

My experience with Kevin is that he is a good investigator and that he decided to come to Turkey, to Istanbul, because he had uncovered something that was big, and he wanted to expose it. Kevin reached out to me to help him solve who kidnapped his employees, who slit one of their throats and who stole the Emerald Dagger. The Topkapi place also plays a role in this case. I am beginning to understand that this case is more than about people being murdered; it is about the history and legend of the Emerald Dagger.

In Kevin's files he talked about the Emerald Dagger and about the history of Istanbul and about the palace and the famous Emerald Dagger. The Topkapi Palace is a historically significant site that was the primary residence of the Ottoman sultans for approximately four hundred years. As I recall from what Kevin told me, the palace complex includes several buildings, courtyards, and gardens, showcasing traditional Ottoman architecture and design.

The Emerald Dagger, according to Kevin's and Ms. Jackson's and other descriptions, is adorned with three large emeralds on the hilt, gold inlay work, and intricate designs, making it one of the most exquisite artifacts from the Ottoman Empire. Whoever stole the dagger I believe also kidnapped Kevin's employees. When we find the employees, we will find the dagger. I really need to have a heart-to-heart, inspector-to-inspector discussion with Kevin.

When Mustafa and I were going through the locker at the Sultan Hotel, we found several documents, and among them was the outline of Operation Izar. Apparently, this group operated underground from 2008 to 2012, stealing art and artifacts from the vast collection of Turkish Ottoman art and artifacts. Selim's name is listed as the leader of this group. In addition, the person who tipped off the police in 2012 by a phone call was never identified, except that he was referred to as "Daylight." According to Kevin's information, the group leader was never caught, and for the past fifteen years, the case has remained open. Over three hundred pieces of art and artifacts were stolen, and regarding the paintings, many of them had a team make fake copies and sell them as the originals. Only three of the original fifteen people were ever caught and went to jail. One of those three, according to the records, was an American who was tried but only spent a year in a Turkish jail and was bailed out by paying an undisclosed amount to a foreign national Swiss company.

When I looked further into the company, I learned that one of their board members was Ms. Elizabeth Jackson and that the Swiss company was the one that the Reverend Janice Turner had worked for in international marketing before she left and went to divinity school to become a minister. Further investigation of the records that Mustafa and I had found disclosed that the American was none other than the Dr. Reverend Sterling Halt, who had been employed by the Turkish government as an inside mole in the Operation Izar investigation.

I found it interesting that this same group of people all were in Istanbul at the same time and that much of the stolen art and artifacts were part of what Mustafa and I discovered in the locker and that, at the same time, the Emerald Dagger is still missing along with Kevin's employees. The pieces of

CHAPTER 17

this case are beginning to fall into place. I now just need to discover or figure out the why. I do believe that Selim was the mastermind behind the thefts and the fakes being created back in 2008 through 2012. I also believe that he was the party who made the call to tip off the Turkish police and that the police referred to him as "Daylight." Selim, according to what Kevin had discovered never spent time in jail. However, when the Emerald Dagger was stolen from the Topkapi's basement and the curator killed Selim became the prime suspect, and according to Kevin, he escaped to the United States to avoid what was happening back in Istanbul.

I also believe that Selim knew who some of the key people were who were involved in the art theft and creating of fake art and that is why he was shot down at the Munich airport. I also believe that Selim was ready to spill the beans so to speak and identify to me all the key players in the theft and in the stealing of the Emerald Dagger. Selim had eluded the law for over ten years, and the questions I must now ask myself are why he resurfaced and what was he after.

Many more questions than answers, but parts of this complex case are starting to come together and to make sense. To solve this complex case, I need to go back to basic investigation techniques. That includes three things: (1) motive, understanding why someone might want to commit the murder (e.g., jealousy, revenge, financial gain); (2) opportunity, establishing whether the suspect had the opportunity to commit the crime (e.g., their whereabouts at the time of the murder); and (3) means, determining if the suspect had the means to commit the crime (e.g., access to the weapon). Let's consider some of the prime suspects: Ms. Elizabeth Jackson, Reverend Michael Cramer, Dr. Reverend Sterling Halt, Kevin Hanes, Nancy Donaldson, and Mr. Jerry Davison.

Nancy, from what I learned, was killed because she had discovered the financial trail of Operation Izar, and she apparently knew something about where the kidnapped employees were being held. So, I can eliminate her as a suspect. Ms. Jackson could have been killed because she also knew who killed Nancy and who killed Selim. Also, it was her money that bailed Dr. Reverend Sterling Halt out of jail, and apparently, she had been perhaps one of the main contacts that the kidnappers were communicating with. So, the reason to murder her could be tied that she was ready to share with me all that she knew. So, it appears that the murder of Ms. Jackson was a planned event so that she could be taken out of the way.

The Reverends Janice Turner and Austin Roper and the Reverend Michael Cramer are still very much engaged in this case as well as Kevin, my friend, and Mr. Davison, the manager of the Hotel Miughaamara. My task now is to figure out if any of these suspects are on the good side of the law or if they all have had something to do with the thefts and the murders. When I consider such things as personal motives, I can't help but consider revenge, past grievances, or perceived wrongs. Jealousy, romantic entanglements or rivalry, and anger, heated conflicts over not being treated fairly. Of course, then there are the financial motives, debts, perhaps insurance fraud and just plain out robbery, the victim targeted because of either the valuable information that they had or the valuables that are a part of their own personal collection.

When I take all these things into consideration almost any of the suspects would fit any of the motives and reasonings. There had to be more, and somehow every time I pondered over this case, it somehow came back to the simple idea that when we find the Emerald Dagger, we find the kidnapped employees and we find the killer. I need to speak with Kevin. I believe I will find him downstairs in the hotel bar, enjoying a late-afternoon cocktail.

CHAPTER 18
KEVIN'S CONFESSION

I made my way to the overstuffed chairs in the lobby. I had been putting off this hard discussion with Kevin, but I could not put it off anymore. Kevin needed to provide me with some hard and truthful answers. My gut feeling told me that he was involved more than what he had led me to believe. Kevin and I had been through a lot over the years. We had solved many cases when we both worked for the Chicago Police Department in the homicide division. Kevin had a keen mind for investigation and good instincts.

I just need to know why he got me involved in this case and what was it that he was hoping that I would uncover. When I look over all the evidence that Mustafa and I have collected, Kevin appears to be involved up to his eyeballs in the mystery and deception that is such a part of this case. Kevin knew that I would solve this case. I doubt if Kevin, when he reached out, had any idea of what I would uncover and how many people would end up losing their lives. Yet I couldn't help but have a gut feeling that Kevin is involved in some larger way other than just being the CEO of the company that was a sponsor of the art show showcasing the Emerald Dagger. In the past few days, Kevin had been avoiding me, and he knew that sooner or later, I would track him down and demand that he tell me the truth.

The elevator stopped, and the doors opened, and Kevin stepped out into a very bustling lobby full of people who were enjoying a late-afternoon wine-and-cheese hour. Kevin survived the room, looking for a possible inspector sighting. There in the far corner of the room, he saw me. I was sitting in one of the overstuffed chairs, having a conversation with an older woman. When Kevin walked closer, he recognized the woman as Ms. Wong, who was the head of housekeeping for the hotel. Ms. Wong recognized Kevin right away and greeted him with, "Hello Kevin. How is the finding of your employees going?"

I didn't have time to have any in-depth conversation with Ms. Wong, as she said, "I have to be on my way." She left, and I stared at Kevin.

He said, "Inspector, we need to talk."

I replied, "Yes, we do."

Kevin invited me to get comfortable in the overstuffed chair that I was sitting in. He took a depth breath and began to talk. He started out by taking me down memory lane and how, back in early 2008, he had been assigned to an international case that involved art and artifacts being stolen from the great treasury that was part of the Otman Empire treasure that the Turkish government was very proud of. Kevin had studied Turkish art and culture at the University of Chicago and had a general base of knowledge. The Turkish government was hoping that some well-placed informants within the art community in Istanbul would help the Turkish secret police to stay informed as to if any criminal activity was happening or about to happen.

I took the job and let the Chicago Police Department know that I was on an international assignment. I spoke up and said, "Yes, I remember that because you and I were working the case in Chicago where a former police officer was being accused of killing and murdering his first and second wives. I was frustrated because I was getting stonewalled by the Chicago Police Department because the policeman being accused was one of our own. I remember feeling very jealous of you because you were being taken off the case."

Kevin went on to state, "I went to Istanbul and soon after arriving I was introduced to two other members of this special task force, the Dr. Reverend Sterling Holt and at the time the international marketing genius, Ms. Janice Turner. We were working in connection with the Turkish government as independent operators and at the same time had direct accountability to the FBI office of international affairs, whose agent in Istanbul at the time was Michale Cramer.

CHAPTER 18

"The three of us were operating as separate agents in a way and were given the tasks to infiltrate what the Turkish government believed was an international art theft ring operation under the code name Operation Izar. The Turkish government believed and had it on good sources that this ring was about to carry out one of the largest art thefts in Turkish history. The government believed that a small group of about fifteen art professional thieves had been able to bribe their way into various art museums in Istanbul and that the thefts would occur on the inside by these various employees who worked at these various museums. All that the Turkish government could tell the three of us that if any of us were to be captured that we would be totally on our own and that any discussion that we were working under cover for the Turkish government would flatly be denied.

"We agreed that once a month at the Hotel Miughaamara, we would meet and share what information we were able to uncover. That if by chance we ran into each other on the street or any other way, we would act as if we didn't know each other. It was the spring of 2008, and all three of us were excited about this undercover opportunity. We set about our mission, and within a few months, the first major art heist occurred at the Topkapi Palace Museum, which was in the basement. The museum officials were not completely sure how many art paintings and artifacts were taken because they had a very out-of-date method for keeping track of the art and artifacts. The prized Emerald Dagger was taken, and the Turkish government was brought into the case. We were asked by the FBI and by the Turkish government to try to infiltrate the theft organization.

"Dr. Revered Sterling Halt was one of the first ones to be able to be asked to be part of the Operation Izar organization. The leader, a man who identified himself as Daylight, reached out to Dr. Halt, and even though they never met face to face, he was invited to join the organization. The three of us continued to have our monthly meetings, but it became harder and harder for the reverend to attend because he was always being watched, and his moves were being recorded. We had found a part of the hotel that was no longer being used in the basement, a series of rooms, and that became our meeting place. Each of us could enter the hotel and escape to the elevator and take it to the basement, walk through a steel door, and on the other side was a series of rooms. Our meeting place became ideal because once inside, it was impossible for anyone to track us because we were underground, and it was impossible to get a signal.

"For the rest of 2008 and into the spring of 2009, our meetings were short, and all that Dr. Reverend Sterling Halt had to report was that the man in charge, Mr. Daylight, had brought in professional artists to start to paint copies of many of the original paintings with the idea that the organization would begin to sell them on the open market or give them back to the museums, having the museum believe that the originals were being returned to them. It was that next spring, 2010, when at one of our monthly meetings, Janice shared that she had been hired by Operation Izar to market and sell artwork and the paintings to international dealers that her company had contacts with since they specialized in international art and artifacts. Month to month the three of us kept up with our meetings, all the time sending reports to the FBI, Michael Cramer, and to the Turkish secret police. Meanwhile the Turkish secret police began to round up and put in jail the many employees of the various art museums who were involved with the art thefts. In the spring of 2012, the secret police were tipped off, by what they describe as a misplaced call. The caller identified himself as Daylight and proceeded to name names of individuals as well as where they could find many of the stolen pieces of art. The Turkish secret police acted quickly, and out of the three hundred pieces of art that had been taken, seventy-five were immediately recovered. In addition, fifteen individuals had been named, and the Turkish police were only able to capture three. One of those three was the Reverend Sterling Halt.

"The reverend was tried by a Turkish court and was sentenced to ten years in prison. He named as coconspirators me, Janice Turner, and Michael Cramer. All three of us were held in jail but released for lack of sufficient evidence. I came back to the Chicago Police Department and went about my work as if nothing had happened. In the fall of 2021, I was contacted by the now Reverend Janice Turner, and she said that Dr. Reverend Sterling Halt had been let out of prison and had reached out to her to see if she would be willing to start up our code operation again to see if we could have justice brought to this art theft and identify the people who were behind the planning and execution of this three-year art theft.

CHAPTER 18

"I was thinking about retiring from the Chicago Police Department, and I was actively looking for some new kind of adventure in my life. I found a small company, Hao Technologies, that did many things, but one of their main programs was a system that museums could use to help them to catalog and track their many pieces of art and artifacts. I interviewed for the job and was hired, and off to Istanbul I went. I saw this business as a real opportunity for me to begin once again find a way to infiltrate the art dealers' market and find out where the other missing art and artifacts were and be able to identify and bring to justice the people who were involved with the largest Turkish art theft.

"Michael Cramer had left the FBI in 2014 and gone back to school to obtain a degree in divinity and was currently serving as a minster for the Unitarian Universalist Church of Los Angeles as their senior pastor. Janice Turner was now a reverend herself in the United Methodist Congregation of Rome, New York. I googled both to see where they were and how their lives had unfolded after the time we spent in Istanbul. I found their contact information online, reached out to both, and said I wanted to get the team back together again. In a surprising turn of events, both said that they were going to be going on a year sabbatical and that they would be interested in finishing the investigative work that they had started years before.

"They agreed to join me in Istanbul that fall. They arrived that fall, and we began our monthly meetings, but there was a new owner and manager of the Hotel Miughaamara, a Mr. Jerry Davison, and he claimed that the part of the hotel where we used to meet had been closed off after the hotel completed its remodel. We called ourselves a group of consultants that specialized in Ottoman art and artifacts, and I explained that the two reverends were both on a sabbatical from their churches and wanted to participate in research in Istanbul all about the Ottoman Empire. Mr. Davison bought my description and opened his hotel to us.

"For the first few months in our monthly meetings, we had nothing to report. Then one day we learned from Mr. Jerry Davison that Ms. Elizabeth Jackson had invested heavily in the Hotel Miughaamara and would be staying for extended period of times at the hotel. Dr. Sterling Halt recognized the name immediately as the person named on the paperwork who paid to have him released from the Turkish prison, several years back in 2013. Reverend Dr. Sterling Halt had never met Ms. Jackson, but he never forgot her name.

"Reverend Janice also remembered her as the contact that when she had infiltrated the Operation Izar. Ms. Jackson was the person that she dealt with to sell the stolen art to and to market the other artifacts. On a side note, about six months before Ms. Jackson appeared and the two reverends, the Emerald Dagger mysterious showed up back at the Topkapi Palace Museum. A lot of fanfare followed, and the Turkish government celebrated that a national treasure had been returned. No one came forth to claim that they had been the one to have found the artifact. All the museums' officials and the Turkish government were just excited to have it returned.

"My Chicago investigating mind told me that there was more to this story and that I needed to somehow find a way to flush out who might have been involved with the theft and with the return. I approached the museum officials and offered to be the main sponsor of an art show where the Emerald Dagger would be the main attraction as well as other pieces of art that had been stolen and returned. At first the museum officials were not interested and were afraid that a show would only lend itself to having the Emerald Dagger taken again for a second time. I flushed out my contact with the Turkish police, only to be told that the person I needed to talk with was a Middle Eastern man by the name of Mustafa. He had been hired by the American Embassy because of his knowledge of Arabic manuscripts and his experience and knowledge of the Islamic customs and Ottoman art and artifacts.

"I met with Mustafa, and we agreed to work together. When I reached out to you, I was in trouble and really feared for my life. Somone had tipped off the leader of the Operation Izar, and they had put a price on my head according to what Mustafa had learned from his contacts with the Turkish secret police. In addition, on the night before the art show was to open, the art curator was murdered, and the Emerald Dagger was stolen, and three of my employees were kidnapped. I called you because I was familiar with your investigating work and knew that you would be persistent and be able to locate the employees and get the Emerald Dagger returned.

"You arrived and I knew that eventually you and I would be sitting down to have this conversation that we are presently having. What I had no way of knowing that the people behind Operation Izar would go to such great

CHAPTER 18

lengths to protect the Emerald Dagger and even murder to prevent the truth from coming out. I am grateful that you are here, and I am anxious to hear all about what you have uncovered, and I believe I know where the kidnapped employees are being held."

I looked directly at my friend Kevin, feeling very relieved that he had explained to me the connections in this case that I knew nothing about. Just then I heard a voice from across the lobby say, "Inspector Sterling, we need to talk." It was Mustafa, and I am sure he had a plan as to how we were going to get into the basement of our hotel.

CHAPTER 19

THE DISCOVERY

Mustafa stood for a minute, and then I asked him to sit down. I was excited to hear what Mustafa was able to arrange with his contact at the Turkish secret police. Mustafa started to speak and became very excited as he started to tell the story of what he had learned. "It seems that the secret police were tipped off from an anonymous caller, late yesterday, that they need to check with you, Inspector Sterling. The caller said that if you wanted to find the kidnapped employees and the Emerald Dagger, check the Hotel Miughaamara in the basement of the closed-off part that isn't used anymore." What I had learned from Kevin is that he and the two Reverends, Cramer and Turner, used to meet in that part of the hotel before Mr. Davison took over as the manager and part owner.

I had asked Ms. Wong in housekeeping if she would take me to that area, and she said no, that Mr. Davison is the only one who has keys and has asked that all employees stay away from that area. Mustafa went on further to explain what was going to happen in the next few hours. They had secured some old blueprints, which showed the plans before the remodeling. The entrance point would be just beyond the main elevator in the basement. The remodel had constructed a fake wall with a double door that when opened leads to the old hallway, which led out to the garage. According to the former architectural plans, there are three connecting rooms that are off to the right of that

CHAPTER 19

door with a single door that leads into a small hallway with three separate rooms, but inside each room the two end ones have doors that lead into the middle one.

According to the records, which had been filed with the city of Istanbul, these rooms were declared hazardous and not available to be used as hotel rooms. The owners, Ms. Elizabeth Jackson and Mr. Jerry Davison, had filed plans stating that the rooms were being sealed off and would not be used except for storage purposes. The date of the filing was a little over a month ago.

Mustafa went on further to explain the plan as it had been explained to him by his informant. The Turkish secret police would inform Mr. Davison that they would be conducting an informal search of the area just as a precaution and that they would be following up on a misplaced call by an informant that stated clearly that they believed that the hostages were being held at the hotel.

Mustafa said that he had told his informant that Inspector Sterling had found a piece of paper stating, "Help us B224." The informant checked with city records, and B224 was the name of the area in the hotel that Mr. Davison and Jackson had filed a permit for the purpose to complete the remodeling of the hotel and close off that part of the hotel.

Kevin spoke up and said, "I wonder if you and I could persuade Mr. Davison to give us a tour of the area just for old times' sake since I used to meet in that same area several months before. It's worth a try just to see what Mr. Davison will do. We have until 8:00 a.m. tomorrow before the secret police are planning their raid. Better yet, Mustafa, do you think you could use your magic to persuade your friend at the front desk to let you borrow the master key for the hotel? I bet that that key would open that door and if the kidnapped employees are there, we could break them out. It is now 5:30 p.m. Let's agree to meet in the basement by the locked door at 6:30 p.m."

We all three shook hands, got up from where we were sitting, and Kevin and I went toward the elevator and Mustafa toward the front desk. Operation Rescue had begun. Kevin appeared to be very anxious and hopeful that the end of this ordeal was in sight. If they were there, that would solve one part of the case, but we were still not completely sure who was the mastermind behind this theft, kidnapping, and the murders.

The elevator door opened, and out stepped Mr. Davison. He greeted us and asked if everything was OK. We responded that we both were concerned about this case and wanted it to be solved soon and have the hostages and the Emerald Dagger returned without any more murders. Mr. Davison looked right at me and said, "Well, Inspector, I have great faith in you that you will figure this out and solve this case." With that Mr. Davison turned to walk toward the front desk, and we both stood in amazement and stepped into the elevator, pushed the button for the basement, and waited as the elevator descended to the floor below.

Within no time at all, we reached the basement, and the doors opened. We quickly got our bearings and looked for the locked door. Much to our surprise, the door was open ajar, and we went through and could see the hallway off to our right where the B224 rooms were located. We decided to wait for Mustafa to meet us with the key, as he had just texted me and said he was on his way with the master key. We heard the elevator ding and went back through the jarred door to meet Mustafa. We met Mustafa as he was stepping out of the elevator. He looked around and had that look of, "What is going on here?" We decided to investigate further and walked down the hallway to the right of the door. There were the three rooms, but the middle room door was wide open. The three of us went inside and looked around.

It was apparent to all three of us that someone had been staying here. There were empty soft drink cans and three beds that looked as if people had been sleeping in them. We checked the mini-refrigerator; it was stocked full of sandwiches, ice cream and packages of cold cuts and fresh fruit and yogurt. It was clear to the three of us that most likely this was the last place that the hostages were being held. We looked around to see if we could find any clues that might lead us to who was doing this and where they might have been taken. We found nothing, and then Kevin remembered that his employee Richard Franklin was a marketing genius and perhaps he left some type of clues on paper of even opened containers.

I looked in the trash and found four opened yogurt containers. On one was written 1459, the other O. Delight, the next, S. Choice, and the last C. Garden. Kevin said knowing Rick and his creative mind, he was giving whoever found these a clue as to where they are or where they are being taken. The

CHAPTER 19

answer was right there before us; all we needed to do was to figure out what the numbers and the letters were referring to.

Kevin begun to think back on all that he knew about Istanbul, and I joined in as well. Mustafa quickly figured out that 0. Delight could be referring to the Ottoman delight. What delight with the Ottoman. Kevin smiled; he had just figured it out. The year 1459 was the year that the Topkapi Palace was built. The palace was the delight of the Ottoman Empire, S. Choice must refer to Sultan's choice, and C. Garden must be the gardens at the palace.

What Richard so creatively told us that they were being taken to the Topkapi Place and most likely being held in an area around the gardens. Written on the bottom of one of the containers was today's date. That means that they must have just been moved. Which stands to reason that someone must have tipped off the kidnappers that we were closing in. We now needed a plan, and Mustafa said we need to tell the secret police what we had learned, and instead of doing a raid on the hotel, they will do it on the palace.

We all three sat down and heaved a big sigh of relief. The end of this case was getting closer, but I still had to figure out the motive, who had the opportunity, and who had the means. My gut feeling told me that Mr. Jerry Davison was up to his eyeballs in this, but I just couldn't see him killing anyone or arranging to have someone killed. Who had the most to gain, who had the opportunity, and who had the means? I would need more time to think through all the events, and somewhere there was a clue that would lead me to who is behind all of this.

CHAPTER 20
MORE FACTS TO UNCOVER

Kevin, Mustafa, and I all sat quietly in room B224. Mustafa spoke first by saying that he would contact the Turkish secret police and tell them that the kidnappers had moved the kidnapped employees to the Topkapi Palace. I spoke up and asked the question, "Whom do we have left, and what is their involvement?"

Kevin said, "We have the two reverends, Turner and Roper, who we know were involved with the original case and trying to bring the accused parties to justice."

Mustafa said, "What about Dr. Reverend Sterling Halt and the Reverend Michael Cramer? Both have ties to the original case and a motive for murder as well as trying to get their hands on the Emerald Dagger."

"Then we have Mr. Jerry Davison, whose hotel the kidnappers used as a place to keep the kidnapped employees, and supposedly only Mr. Davison had a key." I said that it was important that we somehow keep it quiet that we know what we know. We all three continued to sit in silence, and then I spoke up. "What we need is a well-coordinated plan to rescue the kidnapped employees, recover the Emerald Dagger, and identify the mastermind behind the operation." Mustafa once again reminded all of us that the Turkish secret police would be ready to make a raid on the palace; all we needed to do was to coordinate with them.

CHAPTER 20

"What we know is that the three of us had nothing to do with the kidnapping and the taking of the Emerald Dagger. So that means that DR. Reverend Halt, Reverends Cramer, Roper and Turner, as well as Mr. Davison, all are suspects. We do not know what they know, nor do we know if they suspect that we are closing in on this case. We need a plan that will draw all of them to the palace and lead us to the kidnapped employees and to the Emerald Dagger. As I have stated all along, the key to solving this case is to find the Emerald Dagger.

"I have an idea. Kevin, can you put out a press release that a phone tip from an unidentified source has helped the Turkish secret police to recover the Emerald Dagger? In the press release, state that the dagger will be on display starting tomorrow morning after the press conference which is scheduled for 10:00 a.m. sharp at the Topkapi Palace in the open are near the gardens. Mustafa, you check with the secret police and make sure that they have identified and have plain clothes officers at each of the entry point into the open garden area as well as the exit points from the palace.

"Kevin, since you have the most knowledge of the layout of the palace, can you and I this evening and along with Mustafa identify all the possible places that the hostages are being held? I do believe that your creative employee, Richard, gave us a possible clue when he said Sultan's choice."

Kevin spoke up and said, "The Sultan's Choice in Topkapi Palace likely refers to a significant location or exhibit within the palace complex. One of the most notable areas within Topkapi Palace is the harem, which housed the sultan's family and concubines. The harem includes the sultan's apartments, where the sultan's private chambers were located.

"It would seem to me that Richard must have asked questions of his kidnappers so he could provide the clue Sultan's Choice. The only way to find out is to go there and get into the palace and go to that area and see if we can find the hostages. We could provide a diversion in the Imperial Hall, which is close to the Sultan's Choice, and if the kidnapped employees are being guarded, which I doubt that they are, two of us could begin to search the area known as the harem."

Kevin again spoke up and reminded me that the Topkapi Palace is a sprawling complex of low buildings, gardens, pavilions, and courtyards, rather than a single structure. The palace has four courtyards surrounded by high walls, with access becoming more restricted as you move toward the fourth courtyard. The harem is a separate section of the palace. The four courtyards are separated by gates. The first courtyard is the largest and most accessible, while the fourth courtyard is the most private. The palace buildings are mostly one or two stories high.

The palace grounds include gardens and pavilions that stretch down to the sea. The palace is separated from the outside world by a high wall with three large gates and five service gates.

The Hagia Irene, a fourth-century Byzantine church, is in the first courtyard.

The sound of the ding of the elevator made the three of us stand up and stay quiet. We heard footsteps, and then we heard someone calling out, "Janice, are you there?" All three of us stood in silence and tried not to make a sound or a breath. Kevin moved quickly and got behind the open door in our room, and Mustafa and I crouched down behind the overstuffed easy chairs that were in the room. Someone was coming our way, and we didn't know who, but we would wait for the right time to appear. The footsteps continued, and now they were almost right outside the door. The person let out a gasp, and Kevin went into action. He stepped out away from the door and tackled the intruder to the ground.

Mustafa and I appeared, and Kevin lifted the head of the intruder; it was Mr. Davison. He said, "I can explain."

Jerry turned to me and said, "Inspector Sterling, I am involved up to my eyeballs, and I need your help." Jerry went onto explain how when his other hotel almost failed and he ended up selling it, he wasn't sure what he was going to do next. Ms. Jackson had kept in touch with him, and she reached out to me and told me about this hotel in Istanbul and asked if I would like to invest in it and manage it. I needed a change and wanted to start a new life.

"Earlier this year I packed up my life in America and moved to Istanbul. Ms. Jackson welcomed me, and she immediately presented me with some remodeling plans for the hotel. It was some minor changes to the lobby and to the restaurant upstairs and then the closing off these rooms, which were not being used anyway. For the first few months, the construction went as planned, and Ms. Jackson and I got along great. Then about a month ago, she started to change. Instead of being easy to work with, she became more

CHAPTER 20

and more demanding. She became very more engaged with the finances and even suggested that we hire an outsider to review the books and to look at our financial position. I was familiar with Nancy Donaldson, whom I had met as a client at my former hotel. I offered her a job as a consultant, and she gladly accepted. At the same time, Kevin was looking for a financial person as well for his start-up company, so I told him about Nancy, and he offered a position to her as well.

"When Nancy arrived, she went to work for both Kevin and me. Within hours after reviewing the financial books of the hotel, she had lots of questions. Before I officially took over as the hotel manager and owner, Ms. Jackson and another silent partner were operating the hotel. When Nancy started reviewing the records she saw several large financial transactions that were being made to a company entry called Operation Izar. She asked me about it, and I told her that I knew nothing. I told her to talk with Ms. Jackson, and she would be able to provide her with some answers. She did seek out Ms. Jackson, and I do believe that Ms. Jackson answered her questions but wasn't very happy that I had sent Nancy to her. Ms. Jackson made it very clear that any business of the hotel financials that happened before I took over was not my concern. The hotel was in a strong financial position and was making money each month.

"After Nancy spoke with Ms. Jackson, she became somewhat aloof. I had sent Nancy the financial records for the past three years and the code to get into the books that were all online. She had started reviewing them long before she arrived in Istanbul. When she arrived, she went straight to work. Nancy came to me the night before she was killed and expressed concern that the hotel appeared to be engaged with a group of people who were into art theft and forging art masterpieces. She also had found a separate account that Ms. Jackson was keeping that showed three million dollars being deposited about two weeks before Nancy arrived. Nancy expected that the money was from the sale of stolen art and artifacts and that somehow the hotel seemed to be gathering place where the type of individuals in that illegal art trade would meet.

"Nancy was putting together a money trail, and I believe in a short amount of time traced part of the money to individuals who were involved with the art show at the basement of the Topkapi Palace. Nancy had uncovered a plot

109

to steal the Emerald Dagger and was concerned for the safety of Kevin's employees and the dagger itself. Nancy shared all of this with me before she went up to the rooftop restaurant to meet with you Inspector Sterling. I know I should have come to you earlier about all of this, but each time I was going to, you were taken away by following those who were going to lead you to the kidnapped employes and the Emerald Dagger.

"Kevin, I owe you an explanation as well. Ms. Jackson came to me on the night that the Emerald Dagger was stolen and the employees kidnapped and asked me if we could allow the kidnapped employees to stay in the B224 rooms in the basement of the hotel. She explained that Ahmet had come to her and said that he feared for his life and that he had received a threatening message by text that said if he didn't pay up five hundred thousand dollars in two days that he would be taken and have his throat slashed. Nancy arranged to fake a kidnapping of your employees, Kevin, to throw off those who were threating Ahmet. Ms. Jackson and I agreed that the three employees could stay in the basement of the hotel and that they would be safe.

"The plan was put into place, and Ms. Jackson arranged for the employees to be moved to the basement of our hotel. She said it would only be for a little while, perhaps three days at the most. She claimed that she knew who had taken the Emerald Dagger and who was behind the threatening messages. She never shared that information with me. When you arrived, Inspector Sterling, Ms. Jackson was surprised and at the same time worried. She told me that she was making a deal with the people who stole the Emerald Dagger and as soon as she got the dagger back, she would arrange for a way that looked as if the kidnappers were willing to meet and let the kidnaped employees go free and get the Emerald Dagger back to you, Kevin, so it could be displayed in the art show.

"The problem that occurred right before you arrived, Inspector, was that Ahmet had come out of the basement and was upstairs in the lobby of the hotel, and he was spotted and taken immediately, and a few hours later, his body was found at the city train station with his throat slashed.

"Ms. Jackson came to me and informed me that she had taken the Emerald Dagger from Ahmet, who had taken that night before the opening of the show because he had been informed that there was a plot to steal the Emerald Dagger. Ms. Jackson had offered the hotel as one of the sponsors for

CHAPTER 20

the event and had been in conversation with you, Kevin, about coming to opening night.

"So unbeknownst to me, Ms. Jackson had the Emerald Dagger and was trying to blackmail the party that had sent a threating note to Ahmet. She wanted to set up a meeting, so she decided to utilize you, Inspector, as a person who would be interested because you had been asked by Kevin to come to Istanbul and solve the case. What you knew was that three of Kevin's employees had been kidnapped, a valuable artifact had been stolen, and one of the kidnapped employees was found in the city train station with his throat slashed.

"Nancy had put together a plan to draw out the person who was black mailing Ahmet. She knew that they were after the Emerald Dagger and that they were hoping to receive five hundred thousand dollars for it. Nancy had figured out on the plane ride from Munich to Istanbul that whoever had possession of the Emerald Dagger had the power to control the outcome. Nancy, in her research and analyzing both Kevin's and the hotel's financials, discovered that, Kevin, your employee Asel Ozturk was connected to a group calling themselves Operation Izar. He was willing to sell the Emerald Dagger and had paid a consultant a finder's fee of three hundred thousand dollars for consulting services. He had hidden that transaction in service fees for the art show. Nancy had tried to trace where the three hundred thousand dollars was paid, but all that she found was a company called stateman listed as the CEO A. Roper.

"Nancy went to Ms. Jackson and learned that your employees, Kevin, were being held in the basement of the hotel. Nancy came to me and verified that the employees were being held in my hotel. Nancy knew that Ms. Jackson had the dagger in her possession and knew where the kidnapped employees were being housed. Nancy figured out that the name A. Roper referred to the Reverend Austin Roper. Nancy in a short amount of time had figured out that Ms. Jackson was trying to pull a deal with the Emerald Dagger and that the Reverend Austin Roper was trying to get his hands on the Emerald Dagger. She remembered Austin from when she had met him at a ministers' conference that she oversaw.

"Ms. Jackson and Nancy worked out a plan that once you and she arrived at the hotel that she would be the one to meet you and inform you that you could meet the kidnapped employees and recover the Emerald Dagger at the Blue Mosque in the courtyard. In the meantime, I had been contacted by Reverend Janice Turner, who had heard that Kevin had reached out to you, Inspector Sterling, to come to Istanbul to help solve the case. She told me that she had been in touch with Reverend Michael Cramer and that he had been here in Istanbul working on a special assignment in connection with the Turkish secret police. He was working with the police on trying to bring the ringleader of the art thefts from 2008 to 2012 to justice.

"Nancy knew that you and she would be on the same flight and arranged to have a seat next to you in first class. She also arranged with the flight attendant, who was a good friend of hers, to plant the small package in the restroom on the plane and to make sure that you received the package and the note telling you to meet at midnight on the roof of the hotel and you would learn about the kidnapped employees and who had the Emerald Dagger. What Nancy hadn't planned on was that Selim would be murdered in front of your eyes, Inspector, at the Munich airport. Nancy than knew that this simple case had turned into a murder case, and she felt out of her element.

"So, Nancy met you and delivered the message to you and then left you wondering about the message and about the murder you both had witnessed at the Munich airport. According to the video at the hotel, Nancy got into the elevator, and it started its descent to her floor. In the hotel video, on the floors below the roof deck where my residence is and where Ms. Jackson was staying, it clearly shows Ms. Jackson leaving her apartment and taking the elevator up to the roof deck and returning even before Nancy left you, Inspector.

"So, the question I am sure you are trying to figure out is who killed Nancy and why. We know by way of the hotel video security tapes that it couldn't have been Ms. Jackson. I did some investigating on my own and discovered that the elevator that Nancy was on stopped on the fourth floor and a hooded person got on. The video never shows Nancy getting off, but it does show the hooded figure getting off the elevator on the floor below the roof and the elevator continuing to the roof deck. The only way that the elevator could have gone back to the roof deck was when you pushed the button, Inspector, to call for the elevator to come to the roof deck.

"If you remember that next morning, you, Mustafa, and Reverend Michael Cramer followed Nancy's clear instructions to go to the Blue Mosque and

CHAPTER 20

that after noon prayers, you will meet some people in the open courtyard of the Blue Mosque and that you would learn more about the kidnapped employees and where they were at and where you could find the Emerald dagger. Ms. Jackson did not join us on that adventure but said that she had work to complete at the hotel. Nor did the Reverend Sterling Halt.

"The three of you went and were greeted by two people dressed in long ropes and they told you through Mustafa that you that the next day at 4:00 p.m. if you came to the Meridian Tower on the European side, the employees would be returned as well as the Emerald Dagger. Ms. Jackson was informed about the exchange by you Inspector and so the next day you, her and Mustafa and Reverend Michael Cramer made your way to the tower at the agreed time. Mustafa and another took cover in the Meriden tower and that gave them a clear view of the bridge. Ms. Jackson, you, and Kevin made your way onto the bridge to receive the kidnapped employees and to retrieve the Emerald Dagger.

"Everything was going according to the plan, and then Ms. Jackson gets gunned down and you almost get kidnapped. Meanwhile there is no Emerald Dagger nor any employees. Someone had been tipped off and for the life of me murdered Ms. Jackson for a reason, but I still don't know why. At this point I am not sure if I have the dagger, and Ms. Jackson has been murdered. Plus, I have the kidnapped employees staying in the basement of my hotel.

"Late yesterday afternoon I received a phone call that simply said, Inspector Sterling knows and if you want to clear all of this up, bring five hundred thousand dollars and drop it off at the Hagia Irene, a fourth-century Byzantine church, which is in the first courtyard of the Topkapi Palace. Come alone and once you drop off the money go inside the church and on the alter will be a package wrapped in a brown paper bag with a white envelope attached. Open the envelope and there will be instructions as to what you ae to do next. Drop off time is set for 2200. That is the time that the guard at that gate takes his fifteen-minute break. Don't arrive before and don't come after we must make that window to not be noticed."

Mustafa, who had been listening to this whole time to Mr. Jerry Davison talk, said, "We need to contact my contacts with the Turkish secret police and engage them in this planned drop." Kevin, Mr. Davison, and I all agreed with that plan.

I spoke up and said, "Does anyone have any idea or clue as to who the person or persons behind this is?" We all took a long look at each other and wondered. Let the adventure begin. Let's catch this murderer and put an end to this case. We all agreed to gather upstairs in one of the hotel's boardrooms and devise a plan for rescuing the kidnaped employees and taking back the Emerald Dagger.

CHAPTER 21
THE PLAN

We all left the confines of the basement and made our way through the former locked door to the elevator. I pushed the button the elevator opened, and myself, Mustafa, Kevin, and Mr. Davison all got in. We said nothing as the elevator rose to the lobby. In no time the doors opened, and we walked out. Mr. Davison led the way to the hotel boardroom. On the way to the boardroom, I realized that Kevin and I had been involved in rescue operations before with the Chicago Police Department. We both had an advantage regarding putting together a plan. We all sat around the board room table. Mustafa spoke first by pointing out that the Turkish secret police knew the grounds of the Topkapi Palace backward and forward, and they would be a great help in assisting us in carrying out our plan. "Mustafa, can you call your contact right now and bring them up to date on how things have changed?"

"Sure thing, Inspector." Mustafa went to another corner of the room and dialed his contact's cell number.

Mustafa finished his call and reported that the secret police were prepared and that they would be utilizing their drones and their hidden security cameras to monitor the palace's entrances, exits, and local movement pattern of the guards. We knew from the phone call that we had a fifteen-minute window in which to act quickly. The drones would be able to provide information on movement as well as possible places where the employees could be hidden. Since according to Richard's clue, they are most likely being held in the area referred to as the Harem.

"Mustafa, can you have your contract inform the Secret Police that we need them to launch two drones one at 7:30 (21:30) and another at 8:00 p.m. (2200)? Let's plan on setting up a command center, in the basement of the Hagia Irene, a fourth-century Byzantine church. The church is in the first courtyard. I will reach out to Father Christian, who is the priest at that parish and who I knew very well when he was serving at St. Thomas in the Hyde Park community of Chicago. He will open the church for us and allow us to do our thing and will support us in any way that he can.

"Mustafa, can you meet with the Turkish secret police and have them highlight per their own intelligence and surveillance critical areas such as the harem, security control rooms, and the possible location of where the Emerald Dagger is being kept? Timing is everything with this operation. We know that the best time is 8:00 p.m., and that is when the drop is going to take place. We need to create a diversion around 8:10 p.m. in the inner courtyard. That way hopefully we can draw out the kidnappers and zoom in and rescue the kidnapped employees."

I looked at my watch; it was now 5:45 p.m. We all agreed that the plan was to gather outside the large wall at the palace at 7:30 p.m. "The success of this operation will depend upon the element of surprise. Good luck, gentlemen."

I looked at Kevin, Mustafa, and Mr. Davison. No one said a word, and we quietly walked away with a feeling of uneasiness but with a plan that we were all committed to. I stood there pondering the whole situation. There are some key players in this: the reverends, Tuner, Roper, Holt, and Cramer. What part have they played or continue to play? I remembered back on something that I shared with Mustafa, that he is the only one that I feel and believe I can truly trust. Mr. Davison is trying, but I still have a lot of unanswered questions with him, and even with my friend Kevin I am not completely sure that he isn't more involved with this. The one truth is that three murders have occurred, and one of these characters or more is the murderer. This case has always revolved around finding the Emerald Dagger, and it will lead you to the murder. I looked at my watch; it was 6:00 p.m. Time to get going and to put Operation Rescue into place.

CHAPTER 21

I took a deep breath and then another one and begin to walk toward the outside door of the hotel. Suddenly, I stopped dead in my tracks. There was the Reverend Janice Turner walking into the hotel, and right behind her was the Reverend Austin Roper. Janice did not see me and walked right by me, but Reverend Austin spotted me right away and greeted me very abruptly and simply said, "No time to visit" and continued in a hurried state to where Reverend Janice was headed.

I looked over my shoulder and saw both reverends speaking to Mr. Jerry Davison, and from the looks of what I could see, it was quickly turning into a heated conversation. I heard Mr. Davison say in a very stern voice, "Reverend you are way out of line, and I never said I would do that." Reverend Austin just looked on and said nothing, but his body language indicated that he also was upset.

Mr. Davison finally looked over and saw that I was still in the hotel. He yelled my name. "Inspector, can you come over here please?"

I moved at such a fast pace, I almost ran. I looked up and simply said, "What seems to be the problem here?"

Both reverends stood there and said nothing. Reverend Austin finally spoke and said, "I understand that you know where the kidnapped employees are and that you have the Emerald Dagger."

I took a deep breath and simply said, "Where did you ever get an idea like that?" Reverend Janice pulled out of her jeans pocket a note that simply said, "I know you want the Emerald Dagger, and it is safe with the kidnapped employees. If you want to see the employees alive and the dagger, you will meet me at the Hagia Irene, a fourth-century Byzantine church on the far corner of the Topkapi Palace tonight at 8:00 p.m. To release the Emerald Dagger and the employees, you must bring $500,000 in unmarked bills. Come alone and drop the money at the guard station."

The look on my face was one of surprise. Who wrote that note and sent it to Reverend Janice, and why was she singled out? I explained to Reverends Janice and Austin that Mr. Jerry Davison had received a phone call yesterday simply stating that he was to bring $500,000 and drop it off at 8:00 p.m. at the same place. "Reverend Janice and Austin, someone is playing all of us against each other in hope that they will be able to collect the money and be on their way and perhaps not even with the Emerald Dagger."

It was 6:15 p.m., and I shared with the reverends that we had contacted the Turkish secret police, and they would be all around the palace with their plainclothes officers and that they would be launching two drones. All we needed was to launch our operation at 8:00 p.m. and see who shows up. The reverends somewhat agreed and were willing to go along. Mr. Davison indicted that he would prepare two bags with $500,000 in each. Mr. Davison then turned to Reverend Janice and instructed her to drop her bag first and then disappear into the church and hide in the hallway right off the main meeting hall. I asked, "What about your drop, Mr. Davison?" Jerry responded that he would wait five minutes and then drop his bag.

I asked once again, "Is everyone clear with the plan?" Reverend Turner and Roper nodded their heads, and Mr. Davison nodded his as well. The only person that wasn't aware of the second drop was Kevin, since he had already left to make his way to the palace. I made a mental note to myself that I would need to make sure that I informed Kevin with the small change in plans. My list of suspects was narrowing down to Reverend Dr. Sterling Halt and the Reverend Michael Cramer. I hadn't seen ether one for a day or two, yet Mustafa and I learned that both of their names appeared in the paperwork about Operation Izar. I wondered if ether one of them would show up to take the funds. Time would tell, and it was now less than an hour before Operation Rescue would begin.

The two reverends, Mr. Jerry Davison, and I stopped at the hotel bar to have a drink. Mr. Davison stated, "Drinks on the house." The four of us stood there at the end of the bar.

The bartender asked me, "What will you have to drink, Inspector?"

I said I would have my usual, "the Sterling." (It's one of my favorites, Caribbean rum, pineapple juice, a splash of cranberry, and a splash of simple syrup). Janice ordered a dry martini; Austin, a Sex on the Beach; and Mr. Davison a cosmopolitan. The bartender walked away and begin to mix up our drink requests.

He returned first with my drink, "the Sterling," next Mr. Davison's cosmopolitan, then Austin and lastly Janice's. I raised my glass and proposed a toast to the finding of the Emerald Dagger and the return of the kidnapped employees.

CHAPTER 21

The toast was well received, and everyone engaged in small chatter, and when it was 7:15 I announced it was time to start making our way to the palace. Mr. Davison had some leftover monk-dark-brown robes in his office and suggested that everyone wear one. He left us to go get the robes. Within no time at all, he returned and one by one each of them put on the robes and tied the sash across our bodies. I was the last one to robe up and did so very quickly. I looked at all of us. "What a photo opportunity," I thought and couldn't resist taking a photo with my phone.

The ten-minute walk to the palace was uneventful. No one even dared to ask us about our robes, and we all really looked like a group of monks about to go into several weeks of solitary. I looked at my watch; it was 7:30 p.m. Our meeting site was in view, and Kevin and Dr. Reverend Sterling Holt was standing there in regular street clothes, next to Kevin. Mustafa quickly appeared out of the darkness. It was 7:45 p.m., and we were ready to begin. The secret police had just launched their second drone. I made my way to the church and had decided to hide in an area on the chancel that was in a direct sight line to where the meeting drops would occur. It was now 7:55, and the guard outside the church was getting ready to go on break directly at 8:00 p.m. Mustafa had just received a confirmation that the first drone launched had located the kidnapped employees; they were in the area called Sultan's and were being held in the middle apartment.

The plan now was to wait and see who came to pick up the money for each drop. Then the secret police would after the second drop zoom in and surround the person and we would have a suspect with the money, and hopefully while that was happening, the secret police would be able to zoom in and take over the operation and deliver to all of us a suspect. It was now 8:00 p.m. and time for our plans to unfold. We all waited in our assigned places. At eight o'clock Reverend Janice made her way to the church entered inside and made her way to the altar. She looked to the left and then to the right and slowly dropped the bag of money. She got up and looked all around and then made her exit to the hallway right off the sanctuary.

I waited in my hiding place. After what seemed like a long length of time but was only three minutes, I heard the church doors open and heard footsteps making their way to the sanctuary. A hooded figure in a long brown robe quickly made their way down the church aisle, stopped by the altar, looked around, and reached down and picked up the bag of funds. They then turned and quickly exited the church. I thought to myself, "Someone has taken the bait, and all we need to do is to wait for the next drop to see if it gets picked up." We didn't have to wait long. I heard the church door, and it was Mr. Davison making the second drop. He knew where to drop the bag of money, did so, and disappeared down the hallway to wait with Reverend Janice. This time within less than thirty seconds, I heard the church door open again, and I knew that someone was on their way to pick up the second bag of money. Less than thirty seconds later, a robed figure appeared and quickly made their way down the aisle stop in front of the altar quickly reached down, picked up the funds, and turned around and walked with a fast pace out of the church.

In the next thirty seconds, what occurred is still somewhat a bit of a blur. I heard shouts outside of the church. "Stop right now, drop the bag, and put your hands in the air." By the time I got outside the Turkish secret police had surrounded the robed figure and the figure was kneeling on the ground with their hands in the air behind their back. Mustafa appeared out of the darkness and walked up to the robed figure reached down and pulled the hood back and shone a light in the figure's face. Much to everyone's surprise, Mustafa revealed that the rope figure was the Reverend Michael Cramer.

In the commotion a band of the Turkish secret police had quickly invaded the harem place in the palace and were able to free the employees, and they were all coming toward us as Mustafa was speaking. With his hands in hand cuffs was none other than the Dr. Reverend Sterling Holt. I asked for the secret police to bring the two gentlemen inside of the sanctuary of the church and then turned and asked for everyone to join me inside for a discussion.

Mustafa and two secret police officers brought Reverend Dr. Sterling Halt and Reverend Michael Cramer to the front of the sanctuary and set them down in the first pews. The rest of the group made their way to the front of the church and quickly set down behind the two Reverends. I looked out at the group. There were Reverends Austin and Janice, Mr. Davison, Mustafa, and Kevin. Mustafa looked at me, and a big smile came across his face; he knew what was coming next. I looked out at the group assembled before me, paused, and took a deep breath and began my discussion. It was going to be quite a performance.

EPILOGUE
LET THE FACTS SPEAK

Once we were all gathered in the small church, I started by telling them all that it had taken me a while, but I had finally figured this case out and I knew why the murders had occurred and who was the mastermind behind them. I went on to say, "This case has always revolved around the Emerald Dagger and its mysterious hold on everyone who encounters it. Kevin let's start with you. I first got involved with this case because you had reached out to me because your employees had been kidnapped and one of them had been found with his throat slit. In addition, the mysterious Emerald Dagger had been taken from its display at the art show the night before the show was to open. Kevin, you and I had worked cases at the Chicago Police Department for many years, and I knew that you wouldn't have been reaching out to me unless you really needed some help with this case.

"The first unusual thing that occurred was that this gentleman named Selim showed up at my condo building in Chicago and claimed that you had sent him to be my escort to Istanbul. Later on when I was preparing to board the flight to Munich, I learned from you that you had not sent him and fact you had told me that the Turkish secret police were waiting for him to come back into the country so they could change him with the murder of the currier of the museum who had been killed the night that the Emerald Dagger was taken. Then at the Munich airport, Selim is mysteriously gunned down and killed. The question that I had to answer was, how was Selim's murder connected to the other three murders of Ahmet, Nancy, Ms. Jackson? All of them had information about the Emerald Dagger, and all had been involved in one way with Operation Izar.

"Mustafa and I learned that Ahmet had been the informant that had tipped the police by making what was called a misplaced call. One of the fifteen thieves that were never brought to justice was Selim. In fact, many believed that he was the mastermind behind all the art thefts, and it was believed he was putting together another plot to steal the Emerald Dagger.

"His killing at the Munich airport was staged to look like the Munich police working in connection with the Turkish secret police and had been tipped off and they were planning to capture him before he boarded. What appeared to be two police making a call, but I checked into that and learned that neither the Turkish secret police nor the German police knew that Selim was going to be at the Munich airport. I had to ask myself, why would Selim need to be killed? What was the motive? Mustafa and I, going through a treasure trove of documents, learned that Selim was blackmailing someone, and that Selim was threating to expose that person to the Turkish secret police.

"That person was you Dr. Reverend Sterling Holt, wasn't it? You arranged with a contact that Mustafa knows at the Turkish secret police to have Selim killed. You figured that since it happened before I arrived that you could get away with it. But you didn't get away with it did you? Because Reverend Janice Turner found out that you had made the arrangement for his demise. Isn't that right, Janice?" Janice nodded her head as if to agree with what I was saying. "Now I ask you, Dr. Reverend, why was Selim killed?"

The doctor stood with his mouth open and finally spoke, and he said, "When I learned that Selim was the person known as Daylight, I knew that I had something that the Turkish secret police would want. Because he knew of our long-term plan to steal the Emerald Dagger, Selim became a liability rather than an asset."

"So, you had him killed, correct?"

"Yes, Inspector. When Mustafa and I were going over the financial records that Nancy left for us to review, we found questions that she had written in the margins for you Mr. Davison. We learned that the hotel before you took over managing had been receiving cash payments of five hundred thousand dollars every three months. This money we were able to trace to the group Operation Izar. You, Dr. Reverend, were a part of that group. Because of your knowledge of ancient manuscripts and knowledge of Ottoman art and artifacts, you were an asset. That is where you first met Ms. Elizabeth Jackson. A wealthy woman who was a natural buyer and contact for selling Turkish art and Artifacts. Dr. Reverend, she became a client and over the years she purchased over three million dollars in stolen art from your collection of forgeries that were part of the Turkish art thefts from 2008 to 2012.

"Ms. Jackson worked out a deal with you that she would find the international buyers and would take a flat 15 percent of the sale.

"When she came to Istanbul to manage and to check on her investment of the hotel, she ran into Reverends Turner and Austin. The two of you were here along with Reverend Michael Cramer as part of a team that had been hired by the Turkish secret police to infiltrate the Operation Izar team and provide information as to who and where abouts of what and how they were disposing of the stolen art and the forgeries. You, Janice, recognized the Reverend Dr. Sterling Holt and shared that information with the Reverend Austin. You both really wanted to do the right thing and turn him over to the Turkish authorities. You had learned that the hotel had become the place where Ms. Jackson brought together the interested parties and closed the deals. You remembered Ms. Jackson from the time when you and the Reverend Roper along with his deceased partner Reverend Lee were all guests at the Grand Hotel that Mr. Jerry Davison was managing.

"You both went to Ms. Jackson together and told her what you were doing in Istanbul. You told her that you were here doing research about ancient manuscripts and art. She believed you until you Dr. Reverend Sterling Holt informed her that the two of you were working for the Turkish Secret police on a project to infiltrate Operation Izar. Unbeknownst to both of you, Reverend Michael Cramer, you were working with Ms. Jackson on a plan to steal the Emerald Dagger and kidnap three of your employees, Kevin, so that you would have to pay a ransom to get them back. Your plan was to steal the Emerald Dagger the night before the grand opening of the art show. At the same time kidnap three of Kevin's employees from his start-up company and demand a ransom. The plan almost came off without a hitch except Ahmet, one of the employees form Kevin's company, was one of the original groups of Operation Izar and he knew you as part of the team that was working with Operation Izar undercover. You and a group of Turkish nationalists that you hired broke through the security in the basement of the Place and were able to steal the Emerald Dagger. You blindfolded Ahmet, Asel, and Richard who were at the show preparations and reached out to Ms. Elizabeth Jackson as the contact to transport the Emerald Dagger and the kidnapped employees. Ms. Jackson knew of the rooms in the hotel and that would be a safe place to house the employees, and she would be able to keep them safe and away from authorities until you could figure out the ransom.

"Ms. Jackson arranged with you Janice and Austin to transport the kidnaped employees and she promised you a part of the ransom for your efforts. You took the employees to the basement of the hotel. You told Ms. Jackson that the two of you used to meet down there before the hotel was remodeled and that you just wanted to go through the area for old times' sake. He gave you the key and you along with Reverend Cramer and Dr. Reverend Sterling Holt moved the kidnapped employees into their holding home. When you got them, all settled in you took off their blindfolds and that is when Ahmet recognized you, Dr. Reverend Holt. Ahmet didn't say anything to anyone, but you could tell that he knew who you were. You got them all settled for the night and told them that their boss would be paying a ransom and as soon as that was received that they would be let go.

"You had learned from Ms. Jackson that Kevin in the meantime had contacted his friend and colleague, the famous Inspector Sterling, and that he would be arriving in a day or so to take over the case. You knew, Dr. Reverend, that you had to remove any trace of Ahmet saying anything to any authorities about you. So, the next morning you met with Ms. Jackson at the hotel and told her that Ahmet had to be disposed of. She agreed with you and devised a plan to bring him upstairs to the lobby and she would have someone like you, Reverend Austin, be the one to slit his throat. Ms. Jackson left you Dr. Reverend Holt and went to the Hotel Sultan to contact you, Reverend Austin. She did contact you Reverend Austin. Right? "Yes." You got Reverend Janice to come with you to the hotel. You both waited in the hotel lobby until you saw Ahmet. You motioned for him to join you and said that you wanted to go to another place to have some Turkish coffee. You walked behind the hotel and had arranged for a contact from the secret Turkish police to be waiting

EPILOGUE

for you and that police man came up from behind Ahmet and slit his throat. You paid him for his services and then choose to move his body to the main Istanbul train station and leave it there. You called Kevin and told him that his employees were safe and that you would be in touch with information regarding releasing the employees and the Emerald Dagger.

"You both rationalized in your minds that the murder was OK because Ahmet had been part of the fifteen members that had been stealing the art and manuscripts and making forged copies and selling them. You had really intended to share all your information with the Turkish secret police, but that all changed on the day that you found out that I had arrived. You knew because of my excellent investigating techniques that I would eventually uncover what you had done and what you were involved with. Neither one of you could have that happen, so you went to Ms. Jackson and convinced her that it would be in everyone's best interest if you just returned the employees and even the Emerald Dagger. Ms. Jackson agreed, and the plan was simple. The kidnapped employes would be brought to the Maiden's Tower and exchanged and given to Inspector Sterling along with the Emerald Dagger.

"No questions would be asked, and I would close my case and be on my way. To add to the plan, no more lives would have to be taken. All of you agreed to the plan. It was being planned with great precession and the plan seemed to be foolproof. Nancy and I arrived in the morning two days after the kidnapping and the theft of the Emerald Dagger. Ms. Jackson wanted me on the case right away but needed to have something happen that would for sure might shake me up but at least get me solving the case. She reached out to one of her contacts a woman that looked a lot like you Janice and asked her to put together a small package with a note saying, "Meet me on the roof of the hotel at the restaurant and someone will come and meet you and share all and let you know where the Emerald Dagger is and the kidnapped employees." It just so happened that women were a Flight Attendant friend of Nancy's and Nancy had made the same request of her. Nancy knew that Ms. Jackson had asked her friend to construct the same note.

"Unbeknownst to me Nancy had been reviewing the financials of the hotel and of Kevin's start-up company, and she had found large cash payments that had been being paid to the hotel in an account called Operation Izar. Over the course of the year the funds in that account amounted to over three million dollars. This information was not known to Mr. Davison because Ms. Jackson was keeping two separate books. Nancy was an efficient financial adviser, and as soon as she arrived, she sought out you, Mr. Davison, and Ms. Jackson. She started asking all the right questions, and Ms. Jackson started to panic. She knew that Nancy would reveal all that she had learned, and that Ms. Jackson little empire would begin to crumble and possibly along with it all of yours.

"Nancy contacted you first, Mr. Davison, and told you that she had found some irregularities with the financial books at the hotel, and she wanted to ask you about several transaction and several large deposits of funds that seemed to not be recorded anywhere except on the bank statements.

"You called Ms. Jackson and asked her to meet you on the evening that Nancy and I arrived. Ms. Jackson never showed up and that evening at midnight I was waiting at the rooftop restaurant for the party that the note said I was to meet. Much to my surprise, the elevator opened and out steps Nancy. She and I had a rushed conversation, and I could tell that Nancy was upset and not her usual self. Nancy delivered the message that the next day in the afternoon we would meet up with the kidnapped employees and have them returned along with the Emerald Dagger.

"Nancy soon left after she delivered that message and about twenty minutes later when I was waiting for the elevator to come up to the roof Nancy was stabbed and put in the elevator and the elevator was sent to the roof. I was the first to discover Nancy's body. At first, I thought that it might have been Ms. Jackson who killed Nancy, but we checked the surveillance tapes repeatedly, and we saw Ms. Jackson go up the stairs to the roof and come back down all during the time when Nancy was eating dinner with me. However, the surveillance tapes did not show anyone else going up the stairs to the roof. What the tapes shown on another set of tapes was you, Reverend Janice, going into the elevator on the main floor and getting off on the fourth floor. That is Nancy's and my floor.

"When Mustafa and I looked at those tapes, we found a seven-minute gap where the tape is blank. After a lot of consideration, we believed it was blank because someone had blocked the camera. Let me tell you what I think happened. Nancy came down from the roof and got off on the fourth floor and you met her and tricked her into trusting you and then you stabbed her and

EPILOGUE

put her body in the elevator and sent it to the roof. You knew that I would be there and would most likely be the first one to discover the body. You were right I was.

"Once you sent the elevator with Nancy's body in it, you removed the blocks from the cameras and got back on the elevator and took it to the lobby. You simply walked out but, on the way, you ran into Ms. Jackson, and she saw the blood on your hand. She asked you about it and you told her it was an old work injury. She knew better and wondered what it really was from. It became very clear to you, Reverend Janice, that Ms. Jackson had to be stopped.

"You went to Reverend Michael Cramer. Isn't that right, Reverend Michael?"

"Yes, Reverend Janice came to me and together we devised a plan in which we would have Ms. Jackson gunned down. On the other hand, Ms. Jackson was planning with you, Mr. Davison, to release the kidnapped employees and to give you the Emerald Dagger. Right after Nancy had been murdered, Ms. Jackson came to you, Mr. Davison, and informed you that the Emerald dagger as well as the kidnaped employees were in the basement of the hotel. You couldn't afford to have bad publicity for the hotel so you and Ms. Jackson designed the plan that she would release them at the Maiden's Tower, and it would look as if the kidnappers would be the ones releasing them and she would take the Emerald Dagger with her and make it look like the kidnappers had also given back the Emerald Dagger.

"Mr. Davison came to you, Reverends Cramer and Holt, and shared with you that he had learned from Ms. Jackson about the Emerald dagger and where the kidnapped employees were being held. He asked if you along with Mustafa would act as lookouts for the release. What Mr. Davison didn't know was that you Reverend Cramer had already spoken with Reverends Turner and Austin and the three of you had devised a plan to have Ms. Jackson gunned down.

"Both of you played your parts well when Mustafa and I and you, Reverend Cramer, went to the Blue Mosque and received a new message that the next day at 4:00 p.m. we were to meet at the Maiden's Tower and the kidnapped employees, and the emerald dagger would be returned. So, the plan was all set and the next day all that you needed to do was to play your parts, and Ms. Jackson would be killed and there would be no exchange of the kidnapped employees or the Emerald Dagger. With Ms. Jackson out of the way, Nancy's murder would go unsolved, and the Emerald Dagger would still be within reach. What you hadn't counted on was that Mr. Davison knew where the Emerald Dagger was and who had it. Ms. Jackson had left it in the hands of one of Kevin's kidnapped employees none other than Richard Franklin.

"So, on the day of Ms. Jackson's murder, Mustafa, Reverend Cramer, and Kevin all came with me and Ms. Jackson to the Maiden's Tower. You, Dr. Reverend Holt, were not among us and stayed behind. At the time I thought that it was strange that you were not joining us. But you did join us, didn't you? You were in the tower that gave you a clear shot to Ms. Jackson. You took that shot, didn't you, Dr. Reverend?"

"Yes, I did. However, you realized right away that things got messy because I was right there by Ms. Jackson, so you came in a robe and tried to knock me out, but Mustafa saw a figure in a robe coming toward me and stepped in and stopped an attempt on my life. I had the wind knocked out of me and was shaken up a bit and received a cut over my left eye."

"After the murder of Ms. Jackson, Mustafa and I were closing quickly in on Operation Izar, and we were working closely with the Turkish secret police. It became clear to Reverend Janice, and you, Reverend Roper, that the only way to get anything for the Emerald Dagger was to use ransom as a mean to get funds. So, it was you Reverend Roper that made the call to Mr. Davison. You knew that the kidnapped employees were being held in the basement of the hotel, so you dreamed up this plan that would net all three of you over one million dollars, and you were then planning on returning the Emerald Dagger by taking claim for saving the kidnapped employees and for recovering the Emerald Dagger.

"For the plan to work, you would need to make sure that the kidnapped employees got moved from the basement of the hotel back to the palace where you all knew there were rooms in the palace where they could reside until they were rescued. What you didn't know that Mustafa, Mr. Davison, and I had reached out to the secret police for assistance and that they were going to be all over the palace on the night of the money drops. The two of you figured that one would come in and pick up the first drop and then stand in the hallway until the second drop was to happen, and the person in the hallway would leave and go outside and make their way to where the kidnapped employees were being held. It would have worked except the secret

EPILOGUE

police were watching both of you every move. So, the Emerald Dagger is back in its home at the Topkapi Palace Museum.

"Reverend Janice, Reverend Roper, Dr. Reverend Holt, Reverend Cramer will be tried and convicted of murder and conspiracy to commit murder. All of you will be tried for fraud. Kevin and Mr. Jerry Davison, thank you for all your great police work, and of course thank you, Mustafa, for your guidance and constant support and help. This concludes our case. Job well done."

Just then my phone rang, and it was my younger sister, Hannah, calling me from Chicago. She informed me that I needed to come home to Chicago to deal with a family manner. Read about it in my next adventure.

PHOTOS

Maiden's Tower

PHOTOS

Topkapi Palace

Bahia Sophia grand mosque

PHOTOS

Beyoglu- sahkula my

Beyoglu

PHOTOS

blue mosque

Bosmous straight

Chapel on palace grounds

Courtyard of blue mosque

PHOTOS

Faith sarayburnu palace

Front of blue mosque

PHOTOS

Inside the tower's stairwell

Istanbul street

PHOTOS

Madarian tower

Sultan Sophia

ABOUT THE AUTHOR

Reverend Dave Clements is an Ordained Minister in the Unitarian Universalist Faith and served as an Interim Minister at the Cape Town, South Africa Unitarian Church. He is a graduate of Meadville Lombard Theological School. Prior to his call to ministry, he worked as an organizational development consultant overseeing strategic planning, entrepreneurship and fundraising, held several management and director positions, and owned his own consulting business. This is his third book and the second in a series. Other books are, "When the Elephant Laughed", "Inspector Sterling Case of The Wondering Minister" and his newest, "Inspector Sterling Case of The Emerald Dagger."

www.ingramcontent.com/pod-product-compliance
Ingram Content Group UK Ltd.
Pitfield, Milton Keynes, MK11 3LW, UK
UKHW020525080325
455946UK00017B/158